W9-BSD-697

NOBODY'S PERFECT
A Nobody Romance

NOBODY'S PERFECT

•

Gina Ardito

AVALON BOOKS
NEW YORK

FIC
ARD

Published by Avalon Books,
an imprint of Thomas Bouregy & Co., Inc.
New York, NY

Library of Congress Cataloging-in-Publication Data

Ardito, Gina.
  Nobody's perfect / Gina Ardito.
      p. cm.
  ISBN 978-0-8034-7458-1 (hardcover : acid-free paper)
1. Weddings—Planning—Fiction.   2. Disc jockeys—
Fiction.   I. Title.
  PS6301.R43N65 2012
  813'.6—dc23

                                    2011033937

PRINTED IN THE UNITED STATES OF AMERICA
ON ACID-FREE PAPER
BY RR DONNELLEY, HARRISONBURG, VIRGINIA

*For my son, Nick, and his cousin, Shawn.
Thanks for the ideas, guys. Life isn't always perfect,
but it's full of perfect moments.
Enjoy them every chance you get.*

Chapter One

Stuck in morning rush hour traffic on Long Island's Southern State Parkway with her family, Summer Raine Jackson understood the true meaning of torture.

In the passenger seat, younger sister Lyn chattered on and on about Doug Sawyer, the man who'd skied his way into her heart over the winter. "Did I tell you to thank Jeff for asking Doug to be one of his groomsmen, April?"

Directly behind her in the backseat, older sister April, the soon-to-be bride and primary reason for this trek, laughed. "About a thousand times. Jeff's a psychologist, Lyn. He knows you've got an issue with the press. But he also knows I want you in my bridal party."

"I would have found a way to get through it for you," Lyn said. "But having Doug to cling to will make it a whole lot easier."

Beside April, Mom, the family matriarch and official approval-meter, applied coconut-scented balm to her ever-thinning lips. "I still say this is an awful lot of fuss for a second marriage. For both of you."

At the end of the road waited three choices for bridesmaids' dresses. Choosing one style meant to fit the various ages and figures of April's bridal party had been a real challenge. To find three possibilities? Oh, Summer had outdone herself.

But honestly, she had to thank the House of Katya for their spot-on advice. Hopefully, April would like at least one of the gowns. As coordinator for a wedding that had turned

1

into a media event, Summer dreaded disappointing the bride, the groom, or even . . . gulp . . . the public.

In the passenger seat of the Escalade, Lyn reached to switch the radio station, but Summer clamped a hand over her wrist. "Leave it! That's *The Cliff Hanger Show.*"

God knew she needed some kind of comic relief this morning. Only yesterday she'd found a pair of sunglasses in Brad's car. Pink, zebra-striped, with a rhinestone-studded heart in the corner of one lens. Definitely not hers. And unless Brad hid a darker secret than the one she expected, not his either.

With a dramatic sigh, Lyn dropped her hand in her lap. "I can't believe you listen to this creep."

"Cliff Hanger." Mom's disapproval filled the air like a rotten egg smell. "Isn't he one of those disgusting radio personalities who offends everyone and everything?"

"Not really." Summer dared a quick glance in the rearview mirror at her mother's puckered forehead, then refocused on the traffic crawling up a few inches. "Cliff Hanger's the funniest guy on radio these days. His stuff is pretty tame compared to some of those other shock jocks out there." She turned up the radio's volume.

"So, Briana," the host said, "you think your boyfriend might be married and cheating on his wife with you?"

Great. Just what Summer needed. Another reminder that husbands had a tendency to cheat. As if the late nights, runarounds from his receptionist, and new silk boxers in his underwear drawer hadn't already clinched most of her suspicions regarding Brad's lack of fidelity.

"I've got an idea," Cliff continued. "Want me to help you find out the truth?"

"How?" The question came from a tinny voice on the radio, obviously a woman on a speakerphone. Briana, the possible Other Woman.

"Here's what I'm thinking," Cliff replied. "Whaddya say we call him?"

"No!" Briana shouted. "Confronting him won't work. He'll probably lie and say he's not married."

"I'll be clever," Cliff assured her. "You'll see. He won't have any idea he's confessing. Do you have this guy's phone number?"

"I have his work number. He never gave me his home number. That's one of the things that made me suspicious."

Cliff paused, his sigh an audible hiss over the airwaves. "Well, it's almost nine o'clock. Let's see if he's in the office yet."

"Okay. The number is 212—"

"No, no, wait! Don't announce it over the air. I'm gonna put you on hold for a minute. My assistant, Lenny, will get it from you. Lenny, you idiot, are you listening? Pick up the phone and get this bum's name and number. In the meantime, we'll take a quick commercial break."

The jingle for a local pawnbroker filled the Escalade's speaker system.

"I can't believe I'm listening to such drivel," her mother chimed in.

Summer dared another quick glance in the rear-view.

Mom had folded her arms across her bosom in the age-old posture of a critical parent. "Imagine. Some poor unsuspecting soul is about to have his dirty laundry aired on the radio. How humiliating."

"If he's cheating on his wife, he deserves to be humiliated," Summer snapped. "I'll bet his wife is the type of woman who waits on him hand and foot, runs all his errands, keeps a perfect home, and never gave him a reason to stray . . ."

Burned by the heat of three pairs of eyes studying her, Summer let her tirade drift off and pretended to recheck her mirrors. As if a genie had granted her secret wish, the traffic snarl gradually eased around a construction zone where four men sat on the guardrail drinking coffee while one man waved an orange flag.

Your tax dollars at work . . .

Within minutes, they gained momentum and the SUV cruised a bit over the speed limit. Inside the Escalade, though, life remained at a standstill.

Wacky music from a calliope resounded from the car stereo. "And we're back."

Cliff Hanger's voice only added to the tension building inside Summer. Her shoulders stiffened, preparing for the blow from an imaginary punch to the chest. Her jaw ached, and that familiar twitch hovered at the corner of her right eye. But having fought a battle to listen to the show, she'd play it out and feign nonchalance.

"Briana, honey, you there?" Cliff continued.

"Yes, Cliff."

"Good. Now don't say anything. Don't let your boyfriend know you're on the other line. Let me do the talking. All you listeners out there, we're going to bleep out the gentleman's name and the name of his employer. 'Innocent until proven guilty' and all that schmaltz."

The sound of a ringing telephone filled the speakers, followed by the promised bleep when someone picked up.

"Hi, extension *bleeeeep,* please," Cliff said to the office receptionist on the other end of the phone.

"One moment," a nasal voice replied, then dead air.

A long, anxious minute passed. No one spoke.

Then another long bleep pierced the silence, and Cliff's voice barreled around the champagne leather interior. "Is this *bleeeeeep*?"

"Yes. Who's this?"

Upon hearing the man's oh-so-familiar voice, Summer gripped the steering wheel tight enough to crack it. Leather hissed as Mom leaned forward and curled her hands around the driver's seat back. Lyn's head swerved in Summer's direction, staring in open-mouthed surprise. April developed a sudden fascination with the dense tree line that hugged the side of the Parkway. No question, her mother and sisters knew the man's identity as surely as she did.

"Congratulations," Cliff said, laying on a salesman's cadence. "I'm with 1-800-BOUQUET, and you've won a dozen roses for that special lady in your life."

"Oh, yeah? What's the catch?"

"No catch. We're trying to boost our sales with a special promotion. All you have to do is tell us the name and address of the lucky recipient. We'll take it from there."

"Great," Brad replied. "Send them to my wife. Her name is Summer Jackson. . . ."

Summer's heart exploded, and her foot slammed on the brakes. The SUV hurtled to a screeching halt on the road's shoulder, inches from a battered guardrail. The unique musical opening of Lynyrd Skynyrd's "Freebird" suddenly filled the speakers, but her brain barely registered the twangy guitar.

An angry hive of bees filled her ears, buzzing with recriminations. She should've confronted Brad when she'd first suspected the affair. But she'd been too afraid, afraid to hear the words uttered aloud, afraid that once the facts became known, she'd have to face the truth. Her marriage was a sham, a farce, a train wreck.

Hearing that fact confirmed on the radio, on public airwaves, devastated Summer with the effect of two tons of dynamite. To add insult to injury, her mother and sisters had heard the news at the very same time she had.

And of course, in typical fashion, Mom refused to take Summer's plight into account before plunging a stake into the heart of the matter. "Still think that deejay's tame, sweetheart?"

Inside WTXZ Radio's studio, Craig Hartmann, aka Cliff Hanger, slammed the mute button and signaled to his producer to hit the delay. Too late. The woman's name went out over the air. A split second later the opening strains of "Freebird" filled the studio.

"Great, Lenny!" he shouted at the kid on the other side of the glass. "Nice going."

Technically, he was more to blame than Lenny. He should have had his finger on the dump button himself. Another sleepless night with a feverish toddler had thrown off his reflexes.

"Hello? Are you there?" a staticky voice called from the receiver. Obviously, the yutz named Brad still had no idea this was a radio prank. "Did you get my wife's info?"

Time to play *Who's The Bigger Moron*. The guy on the phone? Or himself for screwing up what should have been a simple ten-minute bit?

Okay, think damage control. Maybe this wasn't a major disaster in the making. Maybe he could somehow turn this negative into a positive. Maybe Summer Jackson hadn't heard the broadcast. His demographics slanted more toward young males anyway. Maybe none of her friends or relatives listened to him. He could hope, couldn't he?

"Hello?" the yutz called again.

Jeez, this guy was a real beauty.

Craig punched off the mute button. "Yes, sir, Mr. Jackson, I'm here. Sorry. Could you repeat that address again, please?"

"Oh, sure." He rattled off a street address, no more than half a mile from where Craig lived. Small world, and getting more microscopic all the time.

Without fully knowing why, Craig scribbled Summer Jackson's name and address on a yellow Post-It note. "Got it. Thanks a lot and have a great day." Quickly, he hung up. A second blinking light reminded him Briana waited on hold on another line. While the Van Zandt boys wailed about this bird you cannot tame in the background, he clicked on the next extension. "Briana, you still there?"

"Yes." The single word came out a choked sob. "Are we . . . are we on the air?"

"No. Looks like you got your answer, though, huh?" The minute the words left his mouth, he realized how stupid and insensitive they were. *You're on a roll, genius.*

"Yeah." She sniffed. "Thanks."

Time to salvage something honorable from the cesspool he'd dug today. "Look, Briana. For what it's worth, I'm sorry it worked out this way. At least you found out before you got in over your head."

"You think?" She laughed, a sound more bitter than the

green apple spray he used to keep his dog from chewing on the furniture. "I loved him, Cliff. I mean, I really loved him. I thought Brad was *the one,* you know?"

Aw, jeez. He didn't have time to talk to this kid about her love life. His sidekick, Maureen, usually took care of the gooey stuff. Lucky Maureen had picked the perfect morning to call in sick.

He shot a panicked look at Lenny and stretched out his hands to indicate he needed more time before going back on the air. The kid flashed the okay sign, thumb and index finger curled in a circle. Thank God Lenny wasn't nearly as stupid as Cliff made him out to be on a regular basis.

The on-air Cliff Hanger was the polar opposite of real-life Craig Hartmann. He'd purposely devised the Cliff Hanger persona to keep his public and private lives completely separate. This situation managed to temporarily meld the two men into one. One man who had just ruined two women's lives. And all before nine o'clock on a Monday morning.

The week was off to a terrific start.

Chapter Two

The silence inside the SUV grew so heavy Summer couldn't catch her breath. She'd flipped the radio station to upbeat Top 40, but the mood remained dismal. Finally, after one too many songs about love everlasting or broken hearts, she surrendered and turned off the radio altogether.

"Hmmmph," Mom interjected into the mausoleum on wheels. "I don't understand couples today. Your father and I didn't have these issues. We managed to stay married for twenty-four years without sneaking around or cheating on each other."

Summer's demeanor danced on a wire between depression and rage, strung over a boiling pit of shame. "Yes, but for at least half of those twenty-four years, Dad was usually in some other state or country with Lyn," she retorted.

"All the more excuse for him to cheat." Mom glared over the top of her pink-tinted cat glasses. "But he never did. Not like Brad." Her disapproving stare shot to April. "Or Peter." She sighed. "At least *you* didn't have children, Summer. Honestly. Your father and I had such high hopes for you girls. Not one of you has anything good to show for your marriages."

Summer winced and focused on maneuvering the curve of the exit ramp. Lyn looked down at her hands folded in her lap.

April, however, went on the attack. "You have two beautiful grandchildren from my marriage, Mom."

If Mom heard April—which, since they were seated less

8

than three feet apart, she must have—she ignored the comment. "And now April's going to roll those dice again with Jeffrey."

"His name is Jefferson," April corrected. "Or Jeff. Not Jeffrey."

"Whatever." Mom sighed dramatically. "It would be nice if you had a recent example of a successful married couple to emulate. I always thought Summer and Brad were perfect. Now I see I was wrong."

Please, God, give me ten seconds to rein in my temper. Ten, nine, eight . . .

But Summer had become Mount Etna, churning molten lava beneath the surface. Today was only the ash of her misery magma. Soon she'd have to pretend she didn't hear the sly whispers behind her back from friends and neighbors. She'd be forced to stand tall against the curious looks from merchants she dealt with on a regular basis.

Pulling to a stop at a red light, she stared at the car next to her. In the driver's seat, a bald man with horn-rimmed glasses sipped coffee from a travel mug. He glanced at her, then quickly looked away. Had he heard the broadcast? Did he know *she* was Summer Jackson? Was there something about her that advertised her identity? If he recognized her, would he pity her?

Her stomach somersaulted, and she bit back a groan. She'd never wanted to be a celebrity. She'd grown up with a younger sister made famous on the ski slopes, then faced her older sister's sudden propulsion into the spotlight on that television show where she met Jeff.

Okay, sure. Summer had experienced a few twinges of envy at the lure of the cameras and the articles in glossy magazines. But she hadn't ever really wanted fifteen minutes of fame. And certainly not thanks to her husband's infidelity.

Her insides flipped like a gyroscope. How in the world would she bear this humiliation?

Only April wouldn't say anything. April, who had every right to crow since Summer had given her such a hard time when her marriage fell apart years ago. Lucky for her, the new and improved April, secure in love with her scrumptious doctor, wouldn't dream of declaring "I told you so," or "You never should have married him."

The way Summer herself had when their situations were reversed. April's ex-husband, Peter, had rubbed her nose in his affairs for so long she probably needed rhinoplasty to remove the scars.

The light turned green, and she stepped on the accelerator. Bile burned her throat when she recalled her sanctimonious attitude over the years. She'd give anything to take back every mean-spirited remark. Because, now, she needed a friend in her corner, someone who'd understand what she felt. Who better than the older sister who'd not only waded through these treacherous waters, but had managed to find a successful, happy future on the other side?

"Maybe we should reschedule the dress shopping for a better day?" Lyn dared a sidelong glance at Summer.

Kaboom. Eruption time.

"Like when? The Apocalypse?" She pulled into the parking lot behind a large pink and blue Victorian house with three turrets that thrust out of the slate-tiled roof.

"I just meant that—"

"Look, we're already here. The gowns are waiting. Let's try to salvage something happy out of the day." Anything to get the subject off her marriage and its imminent demise. With the Escalade in park, she turned off the engine and stepped out. Gravel crunched beneath her designer sandals.

April got out beside her and sidled close. "We don't have to do this right now."

In reply, Summer scaled the steps leading to the wraparound porch, where wind chimes jingled on the early-morning breeze. "Yeah, we do. Lyn's only here for a few days, and we can't move forward with the rest of the wedding plans until you've picked the bridesmaids' dresses."

"Bullcookies," April retorted. "In case you haven't noticed, Lyn's in love. So as long as Doug keeps his apartment in Manhattan, she'll come down here any time I ask, and you know it. Bridesmaid shopping gives her an excuse to spend time with her main squeeze."

Summer shrugged. "It's not like I'm in any rush to go home now, anyway."

"Oh, Sum." April sighed. "I'm so sorry."

Summer strode toward the shop. "Me too." She yanked open the door, and the automatic sensors heralded her entrance with a digital version of Wagner's "Bridal March." Teeth gritted, she loitered in the renovated parlor near the antique curio cabinet. Inside the heavy glass doors, a dozen illuminated shelves displayed bridal headpieces glittering with pearls and crystals. April, behind her, toyed with a large, floppy hat piled high with white silk roses and lace ribbons.

Grinning, she slapped it on her head and folded the broad brim around her ears. "What do you think?"

"You'll wear a hat like that over my dead body," Summer managed to say through her tight teeth.

April immediately removed the hat. "Kidding," she said as she placed the lace and silk monstrosity on the curved silver hat stand in the corner. Her hand reached for another, this one even more garish, with blinding yellow daisies along the crown.

"Don't you dare," Summer threatened.

Lyn giggled.

Mom simply stared around the space, frowning. "Where is everyone? I thought we had an appointment, Summer."

As if summoned by the complaint, Katya's assistant, a prissy young man named Sergio, glided into the parlor. When he smiled, his teeth gleamed whiter than snow. The man probably spent every dime of his salary on dental bleaching and tanning salons. "Mrs. Jackson, I'm so sorry to keep you waiting." He pushed a wave of raven black hair from his golden forehead. Lifting both of Summer's hands to his lips, he allowed his melted chocolate eyes to lock on her face, then placed dry kisses on her knuckles.

Under normal circumstances, his insincere flirtations would

have amused her. Too bad for Sergio, she'd had enough of flirtatious men today. She glanced over his shoulder at the crystal and brass wall clock behind him. At barely nine thirty in the morning, the day had already careened down a steep spiral.

When she returned her attention to Sergio, his gaze had moved to her companions. In an accent thick with false French, he murmured, "Which of these lovely ladies is our bride?"

April, standing directly beside Summer, snickered. "He's kidding, right?"

" 'Fraid not." Summer removed her hands from Sergio's oozing grip and pulled April forward. "This is April."

"Avreeeeel . . ." He took her hands, repeated the kiss-kiss thing, then stared at the square-cut diamond on her left ring finger. "*Verrrry niiiice.* You pick this? Or he did?"

"He did."

"Excellent," Sergio replied as he turned the diamond in the overhead miniature track lights. "Strong. Sure of himself. And fully aware his bride is a rare find, eh?"

April flashed Summer her is-this-guy-for-real look. On a nod, Summer turned to the other two women in their party. "Sergio, this is my younger sister, Lyn, and my mother, Susan."

Sergio stepped away from April. "Of course. Ladies, a pleasure to meet you as well. Katya will be with you all shortly. May I offer you a cold beverage in the meantime? We have an excellent array of waters—carbonated *and* spring."

Summer silently polled the group and received head shakes in reply. "No thank you, Sergio. We'll just have a seat in the salon until Katya's ready for us."

"By all means." Bowing, Sergio swept a hand toward the draperied doorway.

Inside the salon, a baby blue circular sofa sat in the center of plush, dark blue carpet. The walls, paneled in a white-washed maple, pulled blues and pinks out of the wood furnishings and gave the room a pending motherhood feeling that always left Summer stone cold and as empty as her womb.

Against the back wall stood a bank of dressing rooms, and beyond the salon, a room filled with mirrors waited to display a spectacularly garbed woman at every angle.

While Lyn and Mom sat on the high-backed sofa, April paced beside Summer. Her sister's hovering only served to make Summer's nerves twitchier. After several runs back and forth across the floor, she finally grabbed April by the elbow. "Trust me. The dresses are perfect. You'll love them."

"I know that," April whispered. "I'm just . . . thinking."

Oh, boy. Summer could just imagine what April was thinking about right now. Probably reliving her past humiliations with Peter, which was *so* contradictory to the way this day should unfold. Today was supposed to be fun, an opportunity to give April all the wonderful moments a bride deserved.

At last, Katya, petite with steel-wool hair and mocha skin, sauntered in from her rear office. "So, the ladies are all here, yes? Let's get started. Soon we'll have another deliriously happy bride."

Another? No.

One would be nice, though.

After Summer dropped off Lyn and their mother, April sat in the passenger seat of the Escalade and watched the broken white lines on the highway whizz by way too fast. She wanted to console her younger sister, to help her sort through the jumbled emotions. After all, who else knew the pain, the humiliation, the self-flagellation Summer was probably experiencing right now? No one. Not the way April did.

Unfortunately, their friendship was too young, too tentative, to withstand a conversation of this magnitude.

She twisted the engagement ring on her finger. Summer had always enjoyed comparing her happy marriage to April's miserable one. Now the tide had turned. April had the secure relationship, the nearly perfect man in Jeff. And Summer? She sighed. Poor Summer.

Should she or shouldn't she? What if she made the wrong

choice? What if Summer was mulling over whether or not to confide in her? What if Summer decided to pull over here on the Long Island Expressway and throw her out?

Well, if she got stranded, she'd have to call Jeff to come pick her up. Wouldn't be the first time he'd had to bail her out of something stupid. And if she explained to him what happened—about Summer and Brad and Cliff Hanger, he'd understand. He always did. She smiled as her favorite four letter phrase came to mind.

WWJD? What Would Jeff Do?

Simple. Jeff would tell her to extend the branch to her sister. Try to help. If Summer decided to leap, she'd have a handhold to grasp. If not, at least April would have done her best. "Sum?" She dared a quick glance, read the dull defeat in her sister's eyes. "Look, I understand if you don't want to talk, but . . . well, I just wanted you to know I'm here if you change your mind. Not just right now, but later today, next week, next month. If you want to vent or cry or tell me what pond scum Brad is, I'm more than willing to listen."

"Actually," Summer replied, her tone brittle, "I'd appreciate it."

Thank God. Her sister had grabbed the branch.

April nodded. "You okay?"

"No." Summer's sigh weighed more than a trainload of circus elephants. "I feel stupid and insignificant and humiliated and angry. . . ."

"And you wonder if the medical examiner can really detect arsenic during an autopsy," April finished for her. "Been there, mailed the postcards."

"What am I going to do, April? I don't even have a real job."

April leaned across the console and threw a light punch into her sister's shoulder. "Sure you do. Rainey-Day-Wife could use someone with your organizational skills. It's not glamorous, and we don't stage the kinds of parties you're used to planning. You'll be dealing with kids." She held up a hand. "I know, I know. You'd rather undergo a double root canal. But it's a temporary gig until you pick yourself up, dust off, and return to the nine-to-five business world you left when you married What's-His-Face."

On a heavy exhale, Summer offered her a wan smile. "Thanks, April. You're . . . God, you're unbelievable."

"What are sisters for?"

Chapter Three

Craig Hartmann sat in his minivan on the quiet side street and watched for any activity from the white center hall colonial with black shutters. Nice house. Perfectly shaped hedges, neatly trimmed and edged lawn, white vinyl fence that no doubt blocked passersby from seeing the pool and hot tub in the backyard, all screamed idyllic. Very nice digs indeed. Which only made Craig's guilt harder to swallow. Summer Jackson seemed to have a sweet, cushy life. Now he might have obliterated it with one stupid radio gag.

Squirming in the gray cloth seat, he tried to convince himself he wasn't a creepy stalker. His conscience would never let him rest until he made sure Summer Jackson was all right. Of course, he had no way of knowing if she was all right based on his parking spot two houses down and across the street. He didn't even know if she was home.

He sighed. This was stupid. He had to leave. The boys had baseball practice, each at a different field, five and a half miles apart, at six o'clock. Which meant immediately after they scrambled off the school bus, homework hour would begin. Then he'd have to get all three kids fed and the boys geared up and dropped off. He sighed. In less than three hours.

Another fast food night. Here, Chelsea had freely given him custody because he had the steadier job, the better schedule to adjust for their sake. Yet lately he'd failed miserably on the skilled parenting front. Maybe he should call that company Maureen told him about. The one that helped

16

parents gain time. God knew he could use a few more hours in the day. Or an extra set of hands.

As he turned the key in his ignition, prepared to drive away, a luxury SUV zipped into the driveway and parked. A tall, slender woman stepped out, slammed the driver's door, and strode toward the front portico. She looked neither right nor left and slipped inside the house too fast for anyone to stop her.

Hmmm . . .

At this stage of the game, five more minutes wouldn't matter. Time to go to plan B. After counting to twenty, he stepped out of the van, walked around to the passenger side, and slid open the door. He'd strapped a dozen perfect fire-and-ice roses, arranged with deep green English ivy and snowy baby's breath in a cut-glass vase, into Madison's car seat.

Inhale, count to ten, pick up the vase, slide the door closed. And we're off . . .

His nerves bounced like balls in a lottery game's tumbler. This could go one of two ways, and he didn't like either of the possible outcomes.

He strolled up the brick walk, past the garden gnome in green jacket and red cap who held a mushroom-shaped sign engraved with the home's address. The goofy sculpture only increased his anxiety. Summer Jackson obviously had a whimsical side. The idea that he might have broken her heart—even by proxy—made him feel lower than worm food. He noted the flourishing tiger lilies and rhododendron, the azaleas that burst into perfect cubes of alternating fuchsia and white. Unlike his own overgrown hedges, his weed-choked lawn littered with bikes and perpetually dying plants, the landscaping here thrived.

Before he lost his nerve, he pushed the doorbell.

Someone opened the door. Someone who looked exactly like how he'd pictured a woman named Summer Jackson. A tall, slender goddess with blond shoulder-length hair. Her pretty green eyes narrowed on the blooms, and her hands shot to her hips.

"Now, which man thinks I'm stupid?"

He blinked, but inside his rib cage, his heart sank. "I'm sorry?"

"Who sent these? My husband or that idiot deejay?"

No more calls; we have a winner. Or more like a loser. "I'm sorry?" he repeated.

"Never mind. It had to be the deejay. Brad wouldn't be stupid enough to cover *his* mistake this way. Look, do me a favor. Take those to St. Cyril's Hospital, go straight up to the fifth floor. Ask the nurses for the loneliest lady in the ward. Bring them to her. Tell her they're from someone who loves her."

Before he could say anything more, she firmly shut the door.

When Brad came home that night, Summer was primed and ready. Her talk with April had bolstered her resolve.

He greeted her with the same "Hey, Sum" and then swooped in for his usual evening hello kiss. "How was your day today?"

"Interesting," she replied. "We went gown shopping for April's wedding."

"Uh-oh." He hung his coat in the closet and turned, a grim smile on his face. "Any casualties?"

One, she thought. But she said nothing, shrugged, and headed into the living room.

"Anything else happen today?" He glanced from the small drop-shelf table near the door to the cocktail table in the living room.

The heartless creep was looking for roses. He still believed his secrets were safe.

Well, she'd disavow him of that notion pretty quick. "What about you? What was *your* day like?"

"The usual. You weren't out all day, were you?"

"No. April loved dress number two, so we were in and out of the bridal shop within an hour. I've been here since a little before noon."

"Anything happen after that? Something come in the mail maybe? Or any kind of package delivery?"

She flashed him a smile more dazzling than a case of price-less diamonds. "You mean, like roses from 1-800-BOUQUET?"

His expression turned smug. "Ah, so they did arrive. You scared me for a minute there. So, where are they? Let me see what my hard-earned dollars bought me from that place."

"There aren't any roses. Never were. Your girlfriend set you up."

He blinked. Once, twice, three times. "What are you talk-ing about?"

Her eyes narrowed until his outline grew fuzzy around the edges. "Your girlfriend, Briana," she reminded him. "You remember her, don't you? She called in to *The Cliff Hanger Show* today. Suspected her boyfriend had lied about being married."

He laughed, feigning amusement, but fear flourished over his expression. "Oh, come on, Sum, where'd you hear some-thing like that? Your mother? One of your sisters? It's ridicu-lous."

"I heard the broadcast. You know how I love *The Cliff Hanger Show*. Imagine my surprise when I heard my hus-band fail the fidelity test by ordering flowers for me from some phony salesman while his girlfriend heard the whole sorry episode on another line. And all for the delight of mil-lions of radio listeners across the country! Why didn't you just post a message on the Jumbotron at the Meadowlands Stadium?"

"I still don't know what you're talking about. I have no girlfriend."

Pain shredded her as he stood there, a look of utter sincer-ity pasted on his face.

He'll lie, April had advised her earlier. *He'll lie so smoothly your heart will fight to believe him. Don't fall for the act. Believe what you know is true, not what your heart hears. Confront him. Make him admit the truth.*

"Give it up, Brad. You've been caught and I've been

humiliated. What I'd like to know is why. What does this Briana have that I don't? I'm assuming she's a lot younger—"

"Age has nothing to do with it."

Ah, almost an admission. A hot knife slid between her ribs, cut deep into her heart. "Then what made her so special?"

No reply.

"What, Brad? If age has nothing to do with you throwing away ten years of marriage, what does? I think I deserve to know where exactly you found me lacking. I've been a pretty good wife, as far as I know, and—"

"She's spontaneous, okay?" he blurted, raking a hand through his thinning hair—obviously the hundred-dollar-per month prescription was a bust. "Like you used to be."

"Spontaneous?" The word refused to permeate her foggy brain. She'd prepared to react to a dozen different arguments he might have made, but lack of spontaneity was never one of them.

"Yes, spontaneous. I can call her at ten at night and she'll meet me for coffee without worrying that she has to get up early the next day for some Heritage Society garden club meeting. She doesn't care if her lipstick's smeared because we made out in the parking lot. Everything in her life doesn't have to be perfect every single minute. Briana embraces chaos and mess and passion. The way you used to." His voice lowered to a whisper. "Do you remember when we were newlyweds? I never knew what to expect when I walked in the door. You'd set up a picnic in the middle of the living room, complete with champagne, candles, rose petals. Now I'm not allowed to set foot in the living room for fear I might track dirt on the white carpet. You keep this house as if it were a museum, and everything in it is some precious relic, to be looked upon but never touched. Including *you*."

Her mouth tasted Sahara dry. Still, she managed to rasp, "Why didn't you say something? Why couldn't you have talked to me?"

His lips tightened, drawing commas deep in his cheeks.

"That's the point, Summer. With Briana I don't have to say anything. She's just . . . *spontaneous*." He strode to the closet and yanked out his coat. "In fact, I think I'll go see her now."

Guilt momentarily stole her thunder, but then anger overtook her. Why should she feel guilty? *She* hadn't cheated. "What makes you think your precious Briana will welcome you after finding out you've lied to her too?"

He shrugged. "I told you. She's spontaneous." Pulling open the front door, he paused to look at her, his face a mixture of solemnity and relief. "For what it's worth, I'm sorry. I'll come back over the weekend to get my stuff."

With the slam of the door, he was gone.

Summer wasted no time mourning her loss. Fury, bitter but inspiring, dogged her steps as she raced upstairs to their shared bedroom. *Spontaneous.* He wanted spontaneous, she'd show him spontaneous.

Flinging open the double closet doors, she studied the neat contents perfectly organized inside. Cashmere sweaters caught her eye first. Oh, yes.

She gathered the rainbow sherbet of colors and carried them into the bathroom, where she dropped them on the floor of the shower stall. She twisted the tap to full hot and let the steaming water cascade on the soft garments.

Back in the bedroom, the next victims were his suit jackets, all organized according to color and season. They soon joined the cashmere swamp in the shower. Under the sink, she found a bottle of cleaner with bleach. She removed the spray trigger and splashed the caustic liquid onto the soggy mess.

His perfectly pressed and folded dress shirts with monogrammed French cuffs she carried downstairs to the kitchen sink. Now what? Unlike the sweaters, soaking the shirts in hot water and bleach wouldn't appease her ravenous appetite for destruction.

Undaunted, she dug around inside her pantry until she found a jar of spaghetti sauce on the bottom shelf. She popped the top and poured the contents all over the pristine pile of white in the sink. After swirling the sauce with a long-handled bamboo spoon for maximum coverage, she tossed the mess into the dryer and turned the temperature gauge to high to let the red stains set in permanently. *Yum, yum.* Scarlet Letter Parmigiana.

For the next hour, she devised new and exciting ways of destroying every garment Brad owned. She flung his dress shoes into the pool, where they floated briefly before sinking eight feet to the bottom. She ran his silk ties through the paper shredder until the blades jammed. All his slacks—wool, khaki, and denim—met their demise on the blades of her gardening shears. The carefully paired dress socks were separated, with one of each pattern taking a suicide plunge into the garbage disposal. The singles were then haphazardly matched—blue argyle with gray stripe, solid brown with black microdot—and returned to his drawer.

At last, her spontaneous destructive streak spotted her holy grail: his golf clubs. Only one thing to do with his favorite sports accessories.

She dragged them downstairs. *Thunk, thunk, thunk.* Out the front door and to the driveway. There she arranged the clubs, one at a time, in a nice even line. Once empty, the bag itself landed in the trash can for tomorrow morning's pickup.

Satisfied with the placement of all the pieces, Summer proceeded into the garage and started up the engine of the Escalade. A shift into reverse and she started driving downward. The golf clubs made a lovely crunching sound as the SUV's massive weight warped their shape. At the bottom, she shifted into drive and ran over them again. Then down again, up again, down again. At least a dozen times in each direction. On her way into the driveway on her final jaunt, she regretted not including his golf shoes with the clubs. Oh, well. After a brief respite and a glass of wine, she'd take his electric sander to his spikes. She still had to go through all the junk in the garage anyway.

Leaving the wreckage glinting under moonlight in the driveway, she returned to the house. While she plotted the next phase in Operation E-Bradicate, she opened a bottle of Pinot Grigio and filled a water goblet. She'd promised April she wouldn't get drunk, but one glass wouldn't hurt. Moving into the den, she sat on the white leather sofa, and her eyes lit on the fireplace. Devious wheels turned in her head.

She was sipping her second glass of wine when Brad stormed into the house.

"Summer!" He strode into the den, where she sat before a roaring fire. In his hands he held a warped nine-iron, the shaft cracked and bent in two different places, the head twisted into an impossible angle, suitable only for some bizarre Alice in Wonderland croquet game. "What have you done to my golf clubs?"

She took another sip of chilled wine before answering. "I showed them my spontaneous side. Whoops. Looks like my fire's dying. Time to throw on a few more logs."

Rising from the couch, she offered him her most innocent smile. While her gaze never left his enraged face, she reached into the open humidor beside her and scooped a handful of imported Dominican cigars from the cedar shelf.

"Summer, don't," he said, extending a pleading hand in her direction.

"Don't what?" Before he could stop her, she tossed the expensive, imported, hand-rolled stink sticks onto the fire. They sparked, and then, beneath a soft *whoosh* and blue flame, ignited, filling the room with their strong odor.

"You've gone insane." Brad reached to pull the humidor away from her.

She rolled it closer, cradling the burl chest as if it were an overlarge shield. "No, darling. That's where you're wrong. I was never more lucid during all the years of our marriage than I am right now. Why'd you come back? Briana threw you out too?"

His eyes narrowed to slits. "She's angry right now, but she'll get over it."

"Ah, yes. That spontaneity factor again. Well, I hope you don't think you're sleeping here tonight."

"Why not? This is my home."

"Correction. This *was* your home. Until you decided to start a spontaneous affair with Briana. But I can be spontaneous too. In fact, I've spent the last few hours being totally spontaneous."

"Totally neurotic is more like it."

Her smile turned rabid. "Cut your losses, get out now, and I won't ruin any more of your personal belongings. Stay here, and I'm liable to take a sledgehammer to your Porsche while you're sleeping."

He shook his head. "You're making a mistake, babe."

"No, I'm correcting the mistake I made ten years ago when I said 'I do.' Get out. *Now.*" To emphasize her point, she rolled the humidor closer to the fire.

"I'm going," he said quickly. "Give me ten minutes to pack."

"You won't need ten minutes. You're making a clean break, Brad. New girlfriend, new golf clubs, new home, new clothes. A whole new start." She tipped the wine glass to her lips, drained the sweet-sour Pinot in one swallow. "You should hurry. I've already begun to live without you."

Chapter Four

Seated inside her tiny cubicle in the main office of Rainey-Day-Wife, Summer struggled to hang up her phone without slamming it in the realtor's ear. Five months after she had tossed him out, Brad had finally found a way to gain the perfect revenge. He'd sold their home out from under her. She had two weeks to "vacate the premises." No amount of persuasion or phone calls would convince the real estate agent to allow her additional time.

Adding a cherry to her mud pie, he'd sold the house at a loss, meaning she couldn't count on receiving any money from the sale. In fact, she and he would wind up owing the mortgage bankers a few thousand dollars each when all was said and done.

Now she'd be stuck working here for longer than she'd originally hoped. April had been wonderful about keeping her in the office, where her secretarial background could re-awaken and shine. Still, the current job market hadn't exactly embraced her. Technology had whizzed forward while she'd loitered as her husband's perfect Stepford Wife. Her once-stellar computer skills were now as obsolete as a dot matrix printer.

Of course, since Brad had dropped his housing bombshell, April had continually hinted at finding her a position that would solve her problem and keep her gainfully employed—a live-in nanny kind of setup. But Summer had no experience dealing with families in stressful situations. She had little experience with families, period. And forget children. Children might as well be aliens from another planet.

What she *loved* was planning April's wedding. She relished every detail, from finding the perfect venue to shopping for the gowns to deciding on the colors of the table linens. These days a new dream tantalized her: to open up her own wedding planning business. Which would require a great deal of capital. Capital she'd hoped to gain from the sale of that stupid house.

Another bubble burst.

God, how she wanted to cry. Taking a deep breath to steady her trembling nerves, she picked up a pen and grabbed a sheet of paper. She'd need to make a few lists. Priority one, a new place to live. Someplace cheap but not a slum. And despite the economic sense of her alternate plan, she would *not* move in with her mother. A studio apartment would be a lot better.

"Summer?" Brenda, April's second-in-command, poked her head around the soft-carpeted cubicle wall. "Everything okay?"

She grabbed a tissue from the tan paisley box at the corner of her desk and sniffed back the tears. "Yeah. I'm fine."

"April needs you."

On a jerky nod, she rose and strode past the other desks to her sister's office.

The door was slightly ajar, and a man's voice filtered through the open space. "I'll double your normal fees. I'm barely hanging on here. My ex is threatening to renegotiate the custody agreement."

The desperation in the man's pleas caught Summer's attention. With a quick rap on the door, she stepped inside.

April looked up and smiled. "Come on in, Sum. Mr. Hartmann, meet Ms. Raine."

April's cat-that-drank-the-cream expression unnerved her, but Summer offered her hand to the seated gentleman, smooth and smiling. "Mr. Hartmann."

When he finally gazed up toward Summer, his vivid blue eyes widened in surprise. "Umm . . . hi."

"Mr. Hartmann is looking for a full-time caregiver for his family. Live-in, but on a temporary basis. I think this position would be perfect for you."

Of course she did. Because April knew Brad had tossed her out on her ear. Unfortunately, despite the dent to her pride, Summer had to face the fact that her big sister was probably right. A live-in position was exactly what she needed. Such a position would offer her a place to hide, lick her wounds, and bank her salary until she could make her real dream come true.

As if she sensed the battle brewing between Summer's logic and dignity, April simply waited with an open stare. Why oh why did April happen to find this manipulative streak when she grew a backbone? Because the full shoulda-woulda-coulda of April's expression bored into Summer's conscience.

Or rather, shouldna-wouldna-couldna. Starting with, she shouldn't have destroyed Brad's property that night. Even if the rat deserved to lose every petty possession he valued more than his marriage.

Finally, the guilt broke her. "Well, of course I'm available for the position." She stole another peek at the man and silently prayed he'd turn her down. "If that's all right with Mr. Hartmann."

"God, yes." So much for a rejection. The guy looked as if she'd just pulled him off the ledge of a sixty-story skyscraper.

"Perfect." Rising, April smoothed the folds of her black jersey skirt, then added, "I'm going to leave you two to work out the particulars. Please take your time. Choosing someone to care for your family isn't like buying a car. Sum, take my seat."

"Thank you," Mr. Hartmann said to April on a deep exhale. "A thousand times, thank you. I think you just saved my life."

"Don't thank me," April replied. "Thank Summer. If she weren't available, I wouldn't have been able to place you until September."

While April pulled the door closed behind her, Summer

sat in the vacated chair. Mr. Hartmann turned around again toward the desk. "Ms. . . . ?" He blinked. "Ms. Raine? Is that what she called you?"

Long accustomed to the snickers, Summer simply smiled. "I know. Summer and April Raine. I lived with the ridicule for the first twenty-five years of my life. After my divorce, given a choice between going back to my silly maiden name or keeping my ex-husband's surname, I chose the lesser of two evils."

"You're divorced?" The defeat in his tone surprised her. Why should her marital status matter to him?

She nodded. "Like fifty percent of the nation and about eighty percent of our clients. Including you. Only you have the additional burden of children. And I'm guessing that's what brought you to us. So how exactly can we help you?"

"Ms. Raine, you have no idea how grateful I am." Although the emotion behind the words conveyed sincerity, his posture suggested his unease. He perched on the edge of his chair as if waiting for the fire alarm to suddenly blare. "I'm at the end of my rope."

"So I heard. Since we'll probably be working together on a regular basis, call me Summer. Now, I just need a few minutes to go over the info you've already provided."

While she reviewed the forms he and April had completed, her gaze kept straying to the man across the desk. On closer inspection, Mr. Hartmann—she glanced at the name on the top page—*Craig* had the kind of looks that would normally make her heart skip a beat. Or ten. The eyes, of course, caught her at first glance. Neon blue, framed with incredibly long lashes, under dark-winged brows in a sculpted face of angles. Dimples winked at the edges of his full lips. Dark hair, with glints of silver at the temples, skimmed his collar. He hadn't shaved, and the scruff around his cheeks and chin only added to his subtle appeal. Wide shoulders stretched the seams of his cream-colored button-down shirt. Before he caught her drooling, she returned her attention to his application.

His home address flashed like a beacon. No farther than

half a mile from her house. God, could she actually remain in that neighborhood? As an employee? Humiliation heated her cheeks.

Beneath the desktop, out of Mr. Hartmann's field of vision, she fisted her hands. *Face it, kiddo. You're out of options.* Unless she wanted to be homeless or under Mom's rigid roof again. No, thanks. So she'd stiffen her spine and deal like a big girl.

Meanwhile, Mr. Hartmann kept staring at his fingers, at the desktop, at some imaginary speck of dust on the carpet. Anywhere but at her. As if she terrified him. Was he shy or something?

Ridiculous. How in the world could a man so exceptionally good-looking be shy? Or maybe he simply feared she might change her mind about taking him on as a client? She'd heard him confess how desperate he was for help from Rainey-Day-Wife. In her experience, parents who played the desperation card here didn't usually exaggerate. Often, they *under*estimated how drastic their problems were.

She folded her arms on the desk and relaxed her posture. "Tell me, what brought you to Rainey-Day-Wife?"

"A co-worker. Her sister is a client. She recommended the service to me a few months ago, but I kept resisting. I kept thinking I had things under control."

Yeah. That was something everybody did. "But . . . ?"

"But I was wrong."

Naturally.

He plucked a paper clip from the acrylic cube full of office supplies on April's desk and batted it between his hands on the polished surface. "You know that old story about the sword over the guy's head?"

She studied his rapidly moving hands, hands with incredibly long, graceful fingers, while her mind played catch-up. "You mean Damocles?"

He pointed the paper clip at her like a baton. "That's him. Well, I not only have a sword over my head, my kids are swinging on it like little Tarzans."

She laughed. "Tell me about your children."

At last, he looked directly at her, his eyes alight with pride, dimples deep and heart-melting. "I have twin boys, Scott and Nathan. They're nine."

Twins. Terrific. She stifled a groan. Twice the mischief in matching packages. "Are they identical?"

"No, thank God. They're tough enough to discipline when I know which one is guilty. If I couldn't tell them apart, I'd be in real trouble. Problem is, one comes up with a hare-brained idea, and the other executes it. I've lost a lot of sleep fearing they'll wind up as bank robbers someday. One will brandish the note for the teller, and the other will wait outside in the getaway car."

Well, at least he didn't think they were perfect little angels. "No wonder you're exhausted. Two nine-year-old boys can be harder to corral than a herd of buffalo high on energy drinks."

He laughed, a rich and throaty sound that reminded Summer of fine red wine, warming her insides. "Yeah, I can vouch for that. Then there's my little girl, Maddie—Madison. She'll be four next month."

"Wow. You really do have your hands full."

His expression grew sheepish, and he returned his focus to his paper clip hockey. "I also have a golden retriever."

She jotted down a quick note on the top page of papers attached to the bright pink plastic clipboard: *dog; twin boys, age nine, Scott and Nathan; girl, Maddie aka Madison, age four.* "Three kids and a big hairy dog. You just keep throwing curveballs at me."

On a deep sigh, he ducked his head. "I'm sorry. Maybe this isn't such a hot idea."

"It's okay. I *love* a challenge. Really." Maybe if she said it often enough, she'd believe it. She considered the work involved with such a large group. Trepidation roused in her veins. Did April really think she could handle this much chaos? "Anything else I should know about? Snakes? Ferrets? A crazy aunt in the attic?"

He grimaced. "Does my father count?"

Summer fought back a blink. "That depends. How much care does he require?"

"None. Well, really, that's not true. He's opinionated and stubborn and a general pain in my butt. He moved in with us after he had a heart attack about five years ago. And he's been a huge help with the kids. Until last month, when he suffered another 'episode,' as his doctor called it. He's back home and can take care of his own needs, but he can no longer handle the kids." He paused in his paper clip game and locked his eyes on hers. "I sincerely doubt he'd do anything to offend you. He's a true gentleman. Just a little old-school in his thinking."

This required another note: *Dad recuperating from cardiac episode; old-school gentleman. Crotchety?* "Okay. Let's get back to the children. What are their schedules like? What kind of child-care arrangement do you have for them currently?"

"Right now I'm on family leave. My dad used to be my child-care arrangement. See, my workday begins really early, like around four A.M. So the kids are always still asleep when I'm up and gone. During the school year, Dad got them out of bed, gave them breakfast, put the boys on the bus. By the time they'd arrive home in the afternoon, I'd be there. And then I'd be with them until bedtime. Now that it's summer"—he paused and offered an apologetic smile, as if reiterating once again the ridiculousness of her name—"the boys attend day camp from nine to three."

Summer, still taking notes, looked up briefly. "And Maddie? Is she in preschool?"

"No. Is that a bad thing?" His glance fell to the paper clip again.

Was there a desktop hockey tournament coming up she didn't know about? She quirked her lips. "Your daughter's four. She should be in some kind of school environment or she'll be too far behind for kindergarten. But we'll figure something out. Tell me about the boys. What are Scott and

Nathan like? Don't sugarcoat. I'll be with them seven days a week, and if you're not honest with me about what to expect, their adjustment period will be a lot tougher. As will mine. So don't play the doting parent with me. Give me warts and flaws as well as virtues. Are they shy? Or boisterous? Do they play outdoor sports? Or do they prefer video games? Tell me about their interests, favorite foods, what excites them."

"Scott's into swimming. He's good. Really good. One of the best on his team. Nate's all football, all the time. And they're both in baseball, on different teams. Naturally, their practices and games always seem to run parallel to each other."

"And across town, no doubt." When he looked up at her, eyes rounded in surprise, she shrugged. "That's a problem we run into often here. It's hard enough to cheer on two different teams on two different fields at the same time. But when one of those fields is miles away from the other, even two-parent households become frazzled and overextended. When the logistics get so screwed up that the simplest decision requires a degree in physics, parents call us."

"Yeah, well, in my case, logistics is just the tip of the iceberg. My ex-wife remarried some kind of bigwig construction giant. He builds stuff all over the world, so they travel a lot. Originally, she signed over custody of the kids because she wanted them to have a stable home life—something she couldn't provide. Me? I've had the same job for years, same company, same house, everything. And like I said, Dad's been with me since his heart attack about five years ago. Unfortunately, as the kids have grown, their interests have become more diverse. I'm splitting myself into pieces, and there's still not enough of me to go around. I made the mistake of telling Chelsea—that's my ex—that I had to bring Maddie to the football field when she was running a low fever a couple of weeks ago. I stayed in the car with her, and she slept the whole time. But that wasn't good enough, in Chelsea's opinion." He sighed. "She has no idea how tough it is to juggle three kids, a job, their school stuff, their extracurricular activities, homework, doctor appointments. Then, add my father into the mix, and it's sheer chaos."

Chaos. Terrific. Just what she needed. Like her life didn't have enough chaos already. "So your ex thinks she can do a better job?"

"She's a stay-at-home wife. The only thing on her daily agenda is the occasional society luncheon or charity fund-raiser in whatever Podunk town they currently live."

A heated flush crept up Summer's neck and dried her throat. She swallowed hard.

"Now she wants to take the kids from me." He leaned across the desk, hands clasped over the brass nameplate, between the dozen framed photos of April's kids and fiancé that littered the top. "Ms. Raine—Summer. I complain about how tough I've got it as a single dad, but honestly? I'd die without my children in my life. They're my whole reason for breathing."

Sweet. And sincere. Despite her dread of dealing with a family on a one-on-one basis, she liked this man, appreciated his commitment to his family. And she wanted to help him.

"Mr. Hartmann, I promise I will do everything in my power to help you. I can't promise your ex-wife won't win custody. That's up to the courts. But I'm in your corner, no matter what. Okay?"

Summer Jackson was in his corner. Somewhere up above, the good Lord held His gut while He rolled on a cloud in uproarious laughter. Summer Jackson who worked for Rainey-Day-Wife was somehow related to the owner of Rainey-Day-Wife. Had Maureen known about that when she'd referred him here? She'd been furious about the 1-800-BOUQUET scam when she'd come back to work three days later. But she'd forgiven him when she'd seen how torn up he was over the whole debacle. Not that he'd forgiven himself.

Now the target of his stupidity sat across from him, a promise to help him still fresh on her lips. Her pretty, very kissable lips.

Craig squirmed in the leather chair. He had to tell Summer who he was.

Oh, yeah, sure. That would be an interesting conversation. *Hey, Summer. Remember a few months ago, when Cliff Hanger broadcast your husband's infidelity across the nation's airwaves? Well, guess what? I'm Cliff Hanger. The guy who single-handedly wrecked your marriage and your life.*

Awful? Yes. But the situation might prove far worse if he said nothing and Summer found out later from someone else. After he and his children had become dependent on her.

"Mr. Hartmann?"

He flinched, then returned his attention to Summer. Her expression conveyed warmth and comfort. She had the loveliest green eyes he'd ever seen. Clear. Pain free.

"Is there anything else you'd like me to know about your children? Or yourself?"

"I'm Cliff Hanger," he suddenly blurted.

She froze. As if he'd just held up Medusa's head, she went from warm woman to stone statue in the blink of an eye. "I beg your pardon?"

"Summer—" At her sharp look, he tried again. "Ms. Raine, I'm sorry. That day . . . when I called your ex-husband on the air . . . ?"

Nothing. She didn't even blink. Simply stared with that deer-in-a-machine-gun-scope expression. Great. He might as well have shot Bambi right between the eyes.

"I'm so sorry," he repeated. "I was sleep-deprived and slow on the delay. I know that's no excuse, and I know I ruined your life and . . ." Shame washed over him, and he looked down at the carpet. "I probably shouldn't have mentioned that day, but I couldn't sit here and pretend I didn't know who you were."

"You tried to deliver roses to me." The accusation came out a hoarse monotone.

"Yes." He batted the paper clip between his palms, a nervous habit he'd developed years ago. On second thought, he picked up the twisted bit of metal and began to straighten it.

"I was hoping you hadn't heard the broadcast and that everything might still work out for you. You have no idea how badly I felt about what happened."

The shell-shocked expression never left her face as she gripped the desk with whitened knuckles and pushed to her feet. "Would you excuse me for a minute?"

Before he could reply, she sped to the door, fumbled with the knob, and quickly strode from the office.

Oh, way to go, Craig. You just blew any chance of keeping your family together. Summer Raine will rescind her offer to work with you, and Rainey-Day-Wife as a whole will reject you. Then, you'll screw up once too often, and Chelsea will swoop in and steal your kids. Along with your entire life.

Once again, the evil alter ego Cliff Hanger had potentially destroyed something precious to Craig Hartmann.

Chapter Five

Minutes after leaving Summer in her office with Mr. Hartmann, realization smacked April right between the eyes. On a panicked screech, she sped to the rear of the building, where her fiancé had his private suite for clients who needed more than time to heal their familial wounds. The busy hive of activity in April's section—the ringing phones and frenetic employees—faded to soothing cream-colored walls with peaceful landscape art and ocean blue carpet. Quiet, calm. April didn't know if her blood pressure lowered thanks to the placid environment, as Jeff insisted, or simply because any minute now she'd see him in person, which always lightened her mood.

As she rounded the corner, Jeff's receptionist, Paige, switched her focus from the open filing cabinet behind her well-organized desk to April. Her smile widened. "Four more weeks," she singsonged.

A thrill rippled through April's blood. In four weeks, she'd become April Raine Prentiss, Mrs. Prentiss, Mrs. Dr. Jeff Prentiss. . . . God, she was worse than a high schooler with a notebook full of married name versions and doodled hearts.

"So?" Paige pulled the pen away from her platinum hair, just above her ear, and jotted a notation into a patient's chart. "All the plans set?"

"I think so," April replied. "Summer's in charge of the details."

Paige shook her head and slid the drawer closed with a

lavender-skirted hip. "You gotta have a lot of faith in her to give her all that control. I wouldn't trust *my* sister. I'd be terrified she'd screw it up."

"Oh, no." April laughed. "*I'm* the screw-up in our family. Summer could organize a three-ring circus."

Another reason this Hartmann job was perfect for her. Because once the wedding was over, Summer would have *way* too much time on her hands. Too much time to sit around and think about Brad, about ways to get even, about the downward turn her life had taken.

April cast a quick glance behind her. Any minute now, Summer would probably come barreling around that corner, aimed for her big sister and a blood feud. On a shaky breath, she returned her gaze to Paige, who now sat in front of her computer monitor. April gestured with a nod at Jeff's closed office door. "Anyone in there with him?"

Paige grinned. "Nope. He's all yours." She flicked a button on her keyboard. "For about thirty minutes."

"Ten will do." April strode to Jeff's office and, with a quick rap of knuckles, opened the door.

If the outside area reflected serenity, Jeff's inner sanctum was nirvana. Soft light, both natural from the wall of long, narrow windows, and artificial from a pair of Tiffany lamps on the cherrywood end tables, washed warm gold over the entire room. A bookcase set into the far wall contained a few medical volumes mixed with the unusual choice of paperback best sellers in various fiction genres. At the end of each shelf, pastel porcelain Lladró figurines posed in different aspects of daily life: a woman shielded her tilted face from the invisible sun with a parasol, a pajama-clad boy dragged a teddy bear behind him, a man reclined on a couch with an open book, children straddled a seesaw, a pair of ballerinas posed in midtwirl, a bride and groom kissed.

The requisite couch, upholstered in chocolate brown, took center stage, but was flanked by cozy mushroom-colored club chairs for the patient who wanted a more casual mien to his or her sessions.

Beyond the interview area sat Jeff at his mahogany partners desk, a hand-carved antique rumored to have once held the quills of Thomas Jefferson. The writing surface was Nile-green leather, the edges embossed in gold. The pedestals, with rounded feet, bore matching Gothic arches and flame patterns to the natural wood grain. No surprise Jeff looked perfect behind this piece of furniture meant for a man of integrity and justice.

She didn't have to say a word. He simply glanced up from the file on his desk, and his face broke into a smile of welcome. "April." He must have noticed her harried appearance because he flipped the manila folder closed. "Everything okay?"

"So far." She glided to where he sat before he could stand and planted a kiss on his forehead.

Wrapping an arm around her waist, he swiveled his chair toward her. *Plop!* She fell into his lap like a ripe piece of fruit from an orchard tree. Sunlight slanted across his face, illuminating his cheeks in a heavenly aura. She didn't attempt to escape. Instead, she settled closer, pressed her ear against his chest and listened to the steadiness of his heartbeat. God, how she loved this man! His embrace communicated love, security, the promise of passion, and all that was good in life.

"Got a minute for your favorite neurotic?"

"A minute, an hour, a lifetime." He nuzzled her neck, sending delicious tremors over the sensitive flesh of her nape.

She sighed dreamily as her bones melted. "How did I get so lucky?"

"Clean living?" he suggested, then chuckled.

Biting back a smile, she ran her fingers through his dark hair. "You make me crazy."

"Then it's a good thing I'm a psychologist. I can treat you at the standard family discount rate once we're married."

"Good. Bill me next month. Right now, I need your stellar advice."

"Shoot," he murmured near her earlobe.

Lovely, lovely distraction. But she steeled herself against

his warm breath and the shivers that tickled her bare arms. She had more pressing issues at the moment. "Summer," she managed on a long exhale.

"Ah." He pulled away with a sigh. "What did Brad the Rat do now?"

"Nothing." She paused, considered for a moment. In all the hubbub of wedding details, had she told him about Summer losing her house? Yes. Of course she had. "This has nothing to do with Brad. This is about what I just did."

He straightened. "Uh-oh."

"Exactly." She craned her neck to look out the glass at the area where Paige sat, now on the telephone. Still quiet. "I figure she'll come careening through the door before too much more time elapses."

"Oh?" His thumb traced her jaw. Languor crept over her. "What happened?"

Running her palms up and down her arms, she shook off the lazy haze. "I found her a live-in position and kinda foisted it on her before she could say no."

"Plead insanity."

"I'm serious." She quirked her lips and arched a brow.

"So am I."

"Okay." She gripped him by the shoulders and leveled a stern gaze his way. "Try this on for size, funny man. The guy who's hiring a live-in? It's Cliff Hanger."

He sucked in a breath, exhaled on a whistle. "Forget insanity. Plead ignorance."

She slapped his shoulder. "Jeff, stop kidding around. I'm in trouble here. With that sale looming over her head, Summer needs a place to stay. Soon. Now. This guy needs a full-time child-care aide. Soon. Now. I assigned a round peg to a round hole. But she's not going to see it that way. She's going to be furious when she realizes who he really is."

"Who he really is?" He blinked several times in succession. "You lost me. You didn't tell her who she'd be working for?"

"Cliff Hanger is an alias. Unlike my mom and dad, Cliff's parents apparently had the good sense to christen him with a normal name."

"Your name is normal."

"Yeah, right. In knock-knock jokes and adult movies, maybe." She rolled her eyes to the ceiling, then back to Jeff. "Anyway, Cliff's application is under his real name, so I didn't put it together right away. While we talked, his voice kinda stuck in my head for some reason. I kept trying to figure it out—where I'd heard him speak before. Then I remembered what he'd written in his employment info. WTXZ Radio. The light went on in the old attic." She tapped her temple. "Unfortunately, the power supply is slow. I'd already assigned the job to Summer before I made the connection. She's not as brain-dead as I am. And she was a big fan of his until *that day.* The longer they talk, the sooner she'll figure it out. When she realizes who Craig Hartmann really is, she'll blow."

"So plead ignorance and outrage."

A strangled cry of frustration escaped her composure. "Jeff, come on. You're killing me. I need advice, not jokes."

"I'm serious. Think about it."

Okay . . .

Ignorance and outrage. Ignorance and outrage. Play dumb, then blow up when Summer confronts her with the truth. Spew before her younger sister could. Yes. If she played her role with enough fervor, she might be able to maneuver Summer into taking the part of the responsible, competent businesswoman. Oh, yes. This could definitely work.

She flung her arms around Jeff's neck. "You." She kissed his cheek. "Are." His other cheek. "A genius." Full on the mouth.

The farther Summer had to search for April, the more steam built up between her ears. By the time she rounded the corner to Jeff's office, she was a runaway freight train. No skinny, blond receptionist in a purple suit stood a chance. Paige, like everyone else, would have to jump off the rails or suffer the bruises.

Oh, Paige tried. "Summer, hold up," she demanded as she scurried from her desk to block Summer's path. The fool had the chutzpah to stretch her arms wide across the door to Jeff's office.

Summer stopped within inches of the receptionist. "Don't make me hurt you, Paige."

Lucky for them both, Paige backed down and backed away, aimed for the phone on her desk. "Will you at least give me a chance to let Jeff and April know you're here?"

Every nerve in Summer's body snapped. "And ruin the surprise? Don't you dare."

She pushed open the door and stepped inside to find April in Jeff's lap, mouth pressed to his. "Have you lost your mind?" She would have loved to slam the door for emphasis, but Jeff had installed air hinges—to prevent patients from that very action.

Still, April's squeak and flinch suggested Summer had caught her sister off guard. Good. She'd keep the balance tipped in her favor.

"Summer?" April asked. "Is something wrong?"

"You could say that." She folded her arms over her chest. "Do you know who that man is?"

"What man?"

"Mr. Hartmann." She blew out an exasperated breath. "God, April, do you always become so brain-dead when you lock lips with Jeff?"

"We prefer to call it 'handicapped,' " Jeff replied.

April giggled like a toddler with a bubble machine. Until Summer communicated murder through her eyes. "Sorry," she mumbled. "Private joke. You see, when Jeff first kissed me when we were in Harmony House—"

"I don't care!"

Another squeak erupted from April. "I'm sorry," she repeated. "Now, what's wrong with Mr. Hartmann?"

"He's Cliff Hanger."

Ka-thump. April shot to her feet so fast, she knocked the cordless phone off the charging station on Jeff's desk. "What?"

"He told me he's really Cliff Hanger."

She picked up the phone and replaced it. "He *told* you? Why on earth would he do that?" She waved a hand. "You know what? It doesn't matter. No way he's going to get away with trying to trick me into providing services to pond scum."

Summer's jaw dropped. She hadn't expected April to leap to her defense so fast. Once again, the new and improved April managed to surprise her. "April, calm down."

"I will *not* calm down." Her voice rose. "He's got a lot of nerve showing up here and asking for my help. Come on, Sum." She strode around the desk, stalked toward the door. "Let's go shred his contract. Then I'll tell him off. Did he honestly think he could pull that stunt on my sister and then expect me to help him out of a jam? Guess again, pal. I hope his wife gets custody now. She's probably more human than that slime."

As Summer witnessed April's tumultuous reaction, her own fury sputtered and died. "April, wait."

"Why? He's still here, isn't he?" April demanded. "Because I want to give him a send-off he'll never forget."

"April?" Jeff said her name in a manner that sounded both calm and forceful to Summer.

April paused, her hand on the doorknob.

"Wouldn't you be better off just handing his case over to another staff member?"

"He hurt my sister," she reminded him sharply. "Why would I want to help him?"

"A, because you've always insisted business and personal lives have to be kept separate." Elbows on the desk, he steepled his fingers, playing the competent psychoanalyst. "And b, because if you help him, he might talk up your business on his radio show."

April's hands shot to her hips. "When exactly did you become so mercenary?"

Jeff shrugged. "I'm just reminding you of your bottom line."

The air thickened with tension, and Summer braced for a coming April storm.

"That's right," her sister snapped. "It's *my* bottom line. So stay out of it."

Neither spoke. The pair stared daggers at each other, and angry sparks charged the room with enough electricity to power a Manhattan high-rise.

Summer, uncomfortable and eager to avoid stepping into the middle of a lovers' spat, shifted her weight from one hip to the other. "That's enough," she said at last. "Both of you. You don't mean what you're saying right now. You're just experiencing wedding jitters and taking out your nerves on each other."

"Whatever," April retorted. "Come on, Sum. Let's go kick that bum outta here."

Summer folded her arms over her chest again, this time with the intent of becoming an immovable object. "No."

April's lashes fluttered in her wide eyes. "What do you mean, no?"

"I hate to say it, but Jeff's right."

He offered her a smile and a nod. "Thank you."

Summer shot up a hand. "Don't get excited, buddy. You're only half right. We're keeping Mr. Hartmann's account, yes. But you're not assigning it to someone else. I need this job and I'm taking it."

April gasped. "But—"

"No buts, April. Cliff Hanger didn't destroy my marriage. Brad did that all on his own. Now go kiss your fiancé and make up. Then we'll go finalize this deal with Mr. Hartmann."

Head bowed, April made her way back to Jeff's desk. He rose to meet her halfway. When they stood a breath apart, she stretched on tiptoe to wrap her arms around his neck. The kiss they shared left Summer satisfied that all fences were mended but bereft and acutely aware of her newly acquired single status.

When the couple didn't pull away after a reasonable amount of time, Summer clapped her hands. "That'll do, kids."

April jerked back, eyes sparkling and cheeks flushed. "Sorry," she murmured. "Let's go."

As they left Jeff's office, April flashed a brilliant smile at Summer. "God, I love that man!"

"I know," she replied blandly.

Chapter Six

On a bright and sunny Sunday afternoon six days later, Summer climbed out of her Escalade in front of a two-story home with pale blue aluminum siding and navy shutters. At one time, the house must have been an L-shaped ranch like many of the other homes in this neighborhood. The original lines were still in existence on the first floor, but the second story, with its more modern arched windows and vaulted ceilings, was obviously a dormer that had been added at a later date.

Pressing the key fob, she locked the Escalade with a quick *beep-beep*. In case of a last-minute reprieve, she planned to keep all her belongings in the back, except for her purse. Wishful thinking, but she'd cling to the last viable thread that another option might reveal itself before she moved in with Craig Hartmann and his family.

Lifting a hand to her forehead, she shaded her eyes from the strong sun. A sense of doom wrapped her like a wet blanket. One deep inhale. *Okay. Let's get this show on the road.*

She sidestepped the two fallen bicycles, the umbrella stroller that held a toddler-sized Baby Dumbo, and the garden hose that snaked across the uneven pavement. The grass, weed-choked and patchy brown, apparently hadn't seen water from that hose for several days. She shook her head and studied the rest of her surroundings. Aside from the dying grass, the only landscaping she could see was the foundation plants—no, scratch that—*the dried-up brown stalks that used to be foundation plants, which desperately needed replacement,* as did the gutters with their dented and askew leaders. A wrought-iron railing bordered the two concrete steps that led to the front door.

Look how drastically her life had changed. Six months ago, she had lived in a house that compared to this place was the Taj Mahal. And yet, like the real Taj Mahal, her former house was nothing more than a beautiful tomb. This home resonated with *life*—not in the garden, of course, but in the clutter and disarray.

A thousand questions buzzed in her head. Could she really do this? Handle two grown men and three children? And a dog? With absolutely no experience? What if she screwed up? What if the children hated her? What if the decent man she met in April's office was just a front and the obnoxious Cliff Hanger was her "real" employer?

Reaching the storm door with a torn screen that served as the home's front entrance, she pressed the bell. No sound echoed from the chimes. She pressed again, this time straining to hear any kind of signal from inside the house. Nope. Silence. Apparently, the bell was broken.

Well, she'd assumed Craig had underestimated his desperation at their first meeting. Now the proof glared at her through dirty windows, dried-out plants, and a dozen other home basics that needed repair or attention.

She knocked. Immediately, a dog's deep bark intruded into the midday stillness. A hand yanked away the striped linen curtain at the bay window on her right, and a dark-haired boy appeared behind the glass.

"Grampaaaaaa?" he called out over the incessant barking. "Some lady's at the door."

The *thunk-thunk* of heavy footfalls erupted, followed by the opening of the front door. *Whump!* A very large yellow dog collided with the screen. On a shriek, Summer stepped back and toddled on the stoop. Mistake number one. She should have opted for sneakers rather than heeled sandals. Regaining her balance, she studied the golden retriever who practically pushed his face through the screen while barking a clear warning to stay away. That explained the condition of the storm door.

"Brandy, get down," a basso voice grumbled, and a man popped out from the shadows to yank the dog away by the collar. He had eyes the same neon blue as his son's, but his hair, though just as thick, shined silver. Despite the time displayed on her watch—three o'clock—the bear of a man wore a red plaid pajama top with black sweatpants. An incongruous addition, a delicate-looking little girl with a tumble of dark curls brushing the straps of a pale yellow nightgown snuggled into one shoulder. The blue-eyed child wore a shy smile on her waif face.

Want zapped Summer in the heart. Never in her life had she craved anything more than to hold this precious little angel. To keep from reaching out to take the ethereal girl, she clutched her Coach bag with both hands. "Hi. I'm Summer Raine, from Rainey-Day-Wife. I have an appointment with your family today. You must be Mr. Hartmann."

"Call me Ken." He swung the storm door open wide. "And come on in, Miss Raine."

When she stepped inside, blessed cool air blasted her face.

"I just put on a fresh pot of coffee, so I hope you'll share a cup with us. Fair warning, though—it's decaf because I'm no longer allowed the hard stuff. Doctor says it increases my heart rate." He leaned forward and winked. "So does a pretty girl, but if he tells me I hafta stop looking, I'll be finding another cardiologist."

With the outside temperature hovering near ninety-five degrees, the last thing she wanted was hot coffee, but good manners insisted she accept her host's offer. And she wouldn't risk alienating her client over such a minor irritant. Instead, she flashed a smile that suggested the idea thrilled her to her pink polished toenails. "That would be wonderful. Thank you so much."

"Don't worry, I'll ice it for you," Ken murmured. "That was a test."

"Oh?" She paused, gauged his expression, and found his face blank. "Did I pass or fail?"

"Don't know yet." Shrugging, he turned away from her. "It's not a one-question test."

In other words, Grandpa didn't approve of her interference here. Forewarned was forearmed, she supposed. She stood in the dark-paneled narrow foyer and glanced at the photos on the wall. The little angel, Madison, in a lime green bikini grinned from a beach, a crude sand castle standing clumsily beside her. Two adorable dark-haired boys wearing baseball uniforms—one in red and black, the other gray and royal blue—showed off shiny gold trophies. Craig Hartmann embraced all three children plus the dog in front of a Christmas tree dripping with candy canes and white lights.

While the photos distracted her, something cold and wet poked underneath her sundress and into her butt. She screeched and whirled to find the dog, its mouth stretched into a canine smile.

"Brandy!" Ken scolded. "Get off the lady. Go lay down."

Nails clicking across the hardwood floor, the blond bimbo of the dog world bounded out of the entry area.

"Sorry about that," Ken said, then jerked his head. "Come on. Everybody else is in the kitchen."

He led her past a cozy living room with a dark brown velvet sectional. Against the far wall, a large flat-screen television and DVD player ruled over some kind of gaming console. Black cords snaked into the corner near a set of floor speakers. Empty DVD cases covered most of the bare floor. In the center of the area rug sat a miniature race-car track and a large pink Victorian-style dollhouse. A dozen naked Barbies ringed the outside. She frowned. Didn't anyone insist these children pick up their toys? No doubt about it, Craig Hartmann needed help. Not only in maintaining order, but in teaching his children responsibility.

On the outskirts of the living room, a staircase led to the second story. They passed a closet door or two, around a corner . . .

There should have been a sign that read WELCOME TO CHAOS CENTRAL.

In a large but cluttered eat-in kitchen, two dark-haired boys sat at an octagon-shaped glass table, bowls of orange macaroni and cheese and tall glasses of chocolate milk before them. While Ken strapped the little girl into a booster seat attached to a third chair, Summer drank in the mess around her.

The same disorganization she'd noted outside showed in here. Sports equipment littered the floor: baseball gloves and caps, a football helmet, a bat bag, and a rainbow of plastic water bottles caged in a black wire holder. Dirty dishes covered every inch of counter space, along with clear plastic canisters of sugary cereals and a box of dog treats.

A reminder ran through her head like a prayer. *I love a challenge, I love a challenge. . . .*

"Craig says you're here to help us."

She looked around at the clutter, the children, the lone man who fussed with the coffeepot, and frowned. "Where *is* Craig?" Had he abandoned her to this whirlwind on day one?

"Dad's in the basement," one of the boys replied, "trying to fix my football pads."

"What's wrong with your pads?" Ken whirled from the coffeemaker. He held a glass carafe filled with liquid the color and consistency of used motor oil.

Mistake number two, Summer. You should have requested ice water. Another glance around the kitchen. *In a hermetically sealed bottle.* She stifled another shiver, but revulsion slipped an icy finger up her spine.

"Dad says the shoulder pads are too big."

Summer thought back to her notes, then pointed thumb and index finger pistol-style at the boy with stick-straight, thick dark hair and bangs that brushed his round, gray eyes. "You're Nate."

"Yeah." He cocked his head. "How'd you know?"

"Your dad told me you love football."

"What else did he tell you?"

"What did he tell you about *me?*" the other boy demanded. In contrast to Nate, Scott's hair curled wildly, and his eyes held more of a smoky blue hue.

"What about me?" the little girl parroted.

Summer held up a hand for silence. "One at a time. Please. He told me about all of you." Scanning the floor, she quickly determined that between the scattered clumps of pet hair and the various sports equipment, her purse would only survive unscathed if she kept it close. She pulled out a chair across from the boys, sat, and clutched the Coach in her lap. "Let me think now . . ." She paused, drawing out the anticipation.

Ken eyed her speculatively as he placed a muddy beverage in a tall glass near her right hand. *Not a one-question test,* she remembered. On barely a glance, she lifted and sipped. Mistake number three. Even with ice, milk, and sugar, the coffee jolted like battery acid. Biting back a grimace, she smiled her thanks at Ken. The first thing she planned to unpack from the SUV was her single-serving coffeemaker system. *If* she stayed.

"Come ooooooooonnnn!" Scott bounced in his chair. "What'd Dad say?"

A sudden awareness filled her senses. The air crackled. A slight hum reverberated beneath her skin as Craig's voice sounded from behind her. "Don't pester Miss Raine, guys. Just eat your lunch. You've got an hour before we're out the door again."

She turned and found him less than a foot away. He looked exhausted, purple rings under those gorgeous eyes, deep lines in his forehead, as if he hadn't slept since the last time she saw him. From one hand dangled a large plastic contraption that reminded her of the upper half of a kiddie suit of armor.

Those were the shoulder pads for Nate? No wonder Craig thought them too big. She couldn't imagine that skinny boy forced to wear a hard plastic straitjacket.

"These should work now," Craig said, and hefted the pads to show Nate. "We'll check 'em after lunch."

"Thanks, Dad."

At last, Craig turned his attention to her. "Summer, thanks for coming. I see you met the gang."

"We were just getting to the introductions."

"Okay, then. Allow me to do the honors. That's Nate on your left, Scott on your right." His arm brushed her shoulder as he pointed to the little angel. "And Maddie over there. Obviously, you met my dad. And everybody, this is Miss Raine—"

"Summer," she corrected.

Clink! Scott dropped his spoon into his empty bowl. "Wait. Your name is Summer Raine?"

Her lips quirked in a smile. " 'Fraid so."

The boys burst into raucous laughter and, after a quick look of puzzlement creased her brow, Maddie joined in. Even Ken loosed a chuckle.

"That's enough," Craig growled, but his mouth twitched.

"Thank you, everyone. I can see I'll receive a great deal of cooperation from this group. Maybe I should just go back to the office. . . ."

She managed to swerve a quarter turn before Craig gripped the chair to stop her.

"No." His hands slid forward to grip her fingers. Tingles skittered up her bare arms. "God, no. Please."

When she grinned, he relaxed but sent a scathing look toward the children. "I want you to be very nice to Miss Raine, guys. She's going to be living here to help take care of us."

Nate picked up a spoonful of macaroni, shoved it in his mouth, and then asked, "Why?"

Summer cringed at the display of orange mush behind his teeth.

"For starters, so you learn not to talk with your mouth full." Craig's eyes narrowed in the boy's direction.

"We'll definitely be spending some time on manners,"

Summer warned the boys. "As well as picking up your toys and getting organized."

Craig cast a sheepish glance around the room. "Sorry. I really wanted to clean up a bit before you got here, but time slipped away from me."

"It's okay," she lied, and surreptitiously pushed the glass of iced battery acid out of reach. "That's why I'm here, right? To make things easier for you. I'd rather base my conclusions on the reality of a bad day than a perfect one. Bad days, in my opinion, are more common."

"Well, they don't get much worse than today."

"My fault," Ken interjected.

"No, it's not," Craig replied.

Sharp looks flew between the two men, the meaning lost on Summer.

"What *did* Dad say about us?" Nate chimed in.

"He said if you continue to lollygag when you should finish lunch, you're going to be late for your ball game," Craig replied, then returned his attention to Summer. "What do you say I take you on the tour while the boys finish up here? Then we'll unpack your belongings and get you settled."

"Sounds like a plan." Pasting a broad smile on her face, Summer rose from her seat. "Let's get started."

Chapter Seven

Craig had to fight the urge to cringe as he looked at the sorry condition of his house and imagined what went through Summer's mind. The kitchen didn't have an empty space for the woman to set down her purse, which stayed clutched in her lap while they talked. He hadn't found a spare five minutes to clean up after breakfast, and now the time was well past two in the afternoon.

As she stood, he took in her floral-print dress, the matching pink shoes and purse. Her hair swept off her face, pinned behind her left ear with a pink rhinestone clip. Her eyes danced like grass in a summer breeze. Summer Raine looked as pretty as a perfect July day.

In contrast, he probably looked like he'd just sobered up after a week-long bender. Apparently, a night spent in the emergency room followed by a hectic day with no sleep could do that to a man.

Last night, while Dad put Maddie to bed, Craig had played a video game with the boys. He didn't know how he'd heard her over the boys' shouts and whoops after each point scored, but Maddie's sudden cries nearly made his heart stop. When he raced into her room, he found his dad trying to calm a hysterical Madison, who clutched her bloody right foot and howled. Four hours later, the emergency room docs finally discharged her after she received half a dozen stitches and a tetanus shot.

The night's excitement and corresponding rush of adrenaline not only killed his chance of sleep, but also destroyed any doubts he'd harbored about hiring Summer. He'd agonized over this decision since he'd left Rainey-Day-Wife's office on Monday. Dad was dead set against it, of course. He hated the idea of strangers taking care of his precious grandchildren. Until last night's drama changed his mind.

Because Maddie had cut herself on hardwood staples Dad had used to restore a corner of her carpeting earlier yesterday. In a rush to clean up, he must have missed one of the strips of sharp steel. It didn't take *CSI* to figure out what had happened next. Dad thought Maddie had fallen asleep and left her room. For whatever reason—a drink of water, a trip to the bathroom—Maddie had leaped out of bed and landed directly on the toothy end of the staples.

"Ummm . . . where do we start?"

Summer's question jolted him back to the present. He blinked and spread his hands wide. "Well, this is the kitchen."

Her lips quirked. "Obviously."

"And I'm guessing you saw the living room when you came in."

"You're two for two."

"Okay, then. Let's start with your apartment."

Her expression changed from mild amusement to surprise. "My apartment?"

"Well, yeah. Where'd you think you'd stay? In the garage?"

"No, but I was expecting a small furnished room, I guess."

"Originally the apartment was my dad's." On that particular point, he and his father had agreed. Best to keep Summer's living space separate from the family's. This way, she'd have her privacy, and the children wouldn't become confused about her role in their lives. "You'll probably want to girlie it up once you're settled."

Her brows arched sharply, and her hands shot to her hips. " 'Girlie it up'?"

Okay. That was stupid. *Note to self: lack of sleep makes you sound like a moron.* "You know what I mean. Dad's not exactly an interior designer. You'll probably want new curtains, some fresh paint, and stuff. I'll help, or pay, or do whatever you need to make it comfortable for you."

"That's really not necessary, but thank you. I have a lot of my personal things in a storage facility nearby. Once I see what I need, I can pull from there." She turned her spring green gaze to his father. "This is all very sweet. But I didn't expect you to give up your place for me."

Dad shrugged. "I didn't."

"But . . ." She faced Craig again, confusion puckering her forehead. "You just said—"

"After his last cardiac episode, Dad moved down to the first floor," Craig explained. "So the apartment's been empty for a few weeks now. When April and I first discussed my needs, she suggested a live-in because of my crazy work hours. I mentioned the apartment, and that pretty much sealed the deal."

Summer frowned. "I bet."

"That's okay, isn't it?" So much for that note to self. *Oh, God. Please don't tell me I've made some colossal mistake that will cause her to turn around and walk away. Not on the first day.*

"It's fine." She waved a dismissive hand, but furrows still etched her brow, and her lips drew into a tight line.

"Hey, Scott," Nate called from the table. "Train wreck." He opened his mouth wide to reveal a cavern full of chewed-up macaroni and cheese. Both boys burst into hyena laughter.

Craig sighed and shook his head. "Come on." He strode out the doorway from the kitchen, aimed toward the staircase. "I'll show you the apartment."

As he climbed the stairs with her close behind, he became aware of the faint smell of roses and vanilla. Summer's perfume. Maybe his father was right. Maybe this was a mistake. He and Dad both had valid reasons to mistrust the opposite sex. First his mother walked out when Craig was only ten years old, then his wife walked out twenty-five years later.

Now he planned to allow this beautiful, smart, sweet-smelling woman unlimited access to him and his kids. What if they all let their guards down and allowed her into their hearts, and then she left? Only Maddie had survived Chelsea's departure virtually unscathed. Because she'd been ten months old at the time. A few weeks of sleepless nights while Craig got his bearings as a single dad and then, *wham*. A new normal for her. The boys, older when Mom moved out, still cried for her some nights. Not as often these days, but still . . .

If that kind of drama happened again? He gritted his teeth.

Summer was an *employee*, nothing more. Everyone else in this house would take their cues from him. So he'd stop noticing how pretty she looked, how her eyes glistened, and how her skin smelled like an English garden. He dared a glance over his shoulder. His eyes locked on hers, and her responsive smile punched him right beneath the rib cage. Air left his lungs in one quick whoosh. He had to grip the handrail to keep from tumbling down the stairs.

Just an employee. *Yeah, right.*

Summer leaned on the faux-granite counter of the breakfast nook inside her new apartment and created a mental list of items she could pull out of storage to help make this place a home. Her new digs had an eat-in kitchen that contained a short wall of cabinets—four up, four down—with two drawers, an electric range, a countertop microwave, and a small refrigerator with attached freezer. Perfect for the newly single woman, the place reeked of loneliness and depression.

The dinette set, a leftover from some 1970s garage sale, consisted of a round, tan-colored Formica table with three matching wheeled chairs in a dull cream and forest green plaid, plus one almost-matching captain's chair in gold and red plaid. An arched window over the sink, framed by beige lace curtains that would always look dirty rather than feminine, allowed a spectacular view of the frosted bathroom window in the house across the street.

As she'd promised herself earlier, the first of her belongings to find a special place in her new home was her coffeemaker.

The blue glow from the heating element soothed her. Yet, at the same time, in this fortress of solitude, the blue glow creeped her out as well. Nothing the first perfect cup of coffee couldn't alleviate. She'd need milk, of course, and her low-calorie sweetener, before she'd actually use the coffeemaker. And some fresh fruit would be nice. In fact, she might as well start a second list. One for what she'd bring from storage, and another for the supermarket.

The *thunk-thunk-thunk* of Craig climbing the stairs drew her gaze to his entrance. Her garment bag was slung over his shoulder, and a box labeled LINENS rode on his hip.

"Bedroom?" he asked.

"Yes, please." She followed him into the taupe-painted bedroom, where a queen-size sleigh bed, a single nightstand, and a matching oak dresser left little room for two people to loiter. Not that the drab colors inspired anyone to get comfortable in this room. Too much brown for Summer's tastes: brown walls, brown furniture, carpet the color of mud, brown-and-gold-striped curtains. At least now she understood his comment about wanting to "girlie things up." A spot of pink or yellow might definitely help cheer the dullness around her.

Unfortunately, with three weeks until April's wedding, home décor would have to wait. More important details took precedence right now. Details like reviewing the final menu with the caterer, confirming the locale of the rehearsal dinner, setting appointments for final fittings, following up with the florist and photographer . . .

She sighed. Time to write list number three.

So much to do, so little time. For now, she'd settle for what the Hartmanns offered and the few items she'd brought with her. Thank God she had her twelve-hundred-thread-count sheets to put on the bed. Their luxurious softness would go a long way toward making her feel more comfortable here.

Craig set the garment bag and box on the bare mattress, then turned to face her. "Ho-kay. Just two boxes left."

"I'll get them." She turned, but Craig grabbed her wrist in a loose clasp.

"Too late. Dad's got 'em."

The warmth of his fingers tingled up to her shoulders. Thoughts of lists and wedding plans scattered as she lost herself in his magnificent eyes. For a moment, she might have stopped breathing. Finally, though, she came back to herself and pulled away.

"Oh, but . . ." She swerved her focus to the doorway, frowning. "Ken shouldn't be carrying anything too heavy."

If Craig noticed her momentary lapse, he didn't react. "Trust me. I gave him the light stuff." He glanced at his watch. "I've got about five minutes before I'm out the door again for Nate's baseball game. You need anything else before I go?"

"What time will you be back?" He cocked his head to study her at a different angle, and she realized she'd probably sounded like a frightened child. "I just meant, I thought I'd make dinner while you're gone," she hurried to explain. "When should I have everything ready?"

He shook his head. "Don't trouble yourself."

"It's no trouble." In fact, the cooking excuse would give her a reason to get started cleaning that disaster of a kitchen.

Craig's expression darkened. "I said don't bother. I'll take care of dinner for my kids, okay? I've done just fine the last few years."

The words pelted her like sleet, and she flinched. "Okay. I'm sorry. I didn't mean to insult you."

"Craig." Ken Hartmann glared from the doorway, her box of coffee singles perched under one arm.

In response, like a chastised child, Craig dipped his head. When he spoke again, he softened his tone. "Just use today to get settled in. Time enough tomorrow for you to start taking over the domestic responsibilities."

With those words, understanding clicked for Summer. A lesson from Rainey-Day-Wife's new employee orientation echoed in her head: *Many parents struggle to relinquish control. Don't engage in a power battle. Offer support quietly, behind the scenes. Eventually, they'll come to realize the value you provide. If you butt heads from the outset, however, the struggle could escalate to a war, with the children as casualties. . . .*

Time for her to regroup. She'd never allow anyone to use those poor, adorable but ill-mannered kids as collateral damage. "I do have to pick up a few things at the supermarket for myself," she replied, calm and even-toned. "Can I get anything for you while I'm there?"

"No, thank you." He pushed past his father and strode out of the room.

On a sigh, Summer sank onto the edge of the mattress. *We're off to a fabulous start.*

"My fault," Ken grumbled. "Craig's stretched to his limits right now because of last night."

She looked up, studied the solemn expression on Ken's face. "What happened last night?"

He shrugged. "Maddie had a little accident. It's not important, really. Just so long as you know Craig's not always such a b—" He stopped short, doubled back. "Such a bear. It has nothing to do with you. Believe me, he's grateful you're here. And frankly, so am I."

She offered a tired smile. "Thank you."

"No sweat." He hefted the box under his arm. "Tell you what. I'm gonna put this on your counter. If your offer to pick up a few items from the market still stands, I'll grill for dinner. Deal?" He held out his hand.

Rising, she clasped his fingers and shook on it. "Deal."

"Good." He tapped the box of coffee singles. "Now, fix me a cup of high test, and we'll put together a shopping list."

She wagged a finger. "Decaf for you."

"Okay, okay." Ken grinned. "Nurse Ratched."

Maybe things would work out here after all.

Chapter Eight

After an uneventful but successful trip to the supermarket, Summer pulled into the driveway.

Instantly, Ken popped out the front door with Scott. "Can we help?"

She clicked the trunk release on her key fob. "You bet. The plastic bags go in your kitchen, the canvas ones are mine."

"Scott," Ken directed, "you get ours and I'll take Summer's."

"Oh, no. I'll take my own."

"You wouldn't prevent an old man from doing a pretty lady a favor now, would you?"

"Well, no, but your heart—"

"Isn't going to give out from a few bags of groceries. You just get the doors and let us he-men take care of the heavy stuff. Right, Scott?"

"Whatever you say, Gramps." He hefted three of the plastic bags in one hand and nearly spilled the apples all over the driveway.

"Easy there," Ken said as he grabbed the off-balance bag. "We can make two trips if we have to."

"Or I can take a bag or two," Summer suggested.

"No way. In this household, ladies do not schlep heavy bags."

"Even the hired help?"

"Not a friend who's helping us out in our time of need," Ken clarified.

She pursed her lips. *Hmmm . . .* not exactly the way Craig

had made her feel with his remark about taking care of his family.

As Scott took off toward the front door with his share of groceries, Ken murmured, "Don't let my son's bark scare you off. He's under a lot of stress right now between me, the kids, and his ex. He'll come around, I promise."

"I'll remember that."

"Good. Did you get everything I asked for?"

"Yes and no."

"You didn't get veggie burgers or tofu, did you? I don't care what my doctor says—if I'm going to die anyway, I'm going with a smile on my face and the juice of real meat on my lips."

"I got real meat. Turkey. I'll marinate it for an hour or two, and you won't know the difference. Trust me. You'll love it."

His expression turned distrustful. "We'll see . . ."

They entered the house, and Ken shouted toward the kitchen, "Scott, start putting those groceries away while I help Summer upstairs."

Thinking about the condition of the downstairs kitchen, she toyed with the idea of asking Ken to help there. She could handle putting away the meager groceries she'd picked up: milk, sweetener, fruit. Taking control of the disaster area the Hartmanns called a kitchen was a bigger obstacle. But she'd manage. As she climbed the stairs to her apartment, she made a mental list. First stop, the cluttered counters. Then the dishes. Last but not least, the floor. And all before she could start preparing the side dishes for tonight's dinner.

I love a challenge, she reminded herself.

Craig returned home three hours later, sweaty, irritable, and exhausted. Still, his senses recognized all the signs of a backyard barbecue in full swing. The aroma of grilling meat tantalized his stomach. Maddie's giggles danced on the evening air.

Nate, beside him, inhaled and grinned. "Cool. A cookout. I'm starving."

Craig's posture stiffened. Summer was crossing the line already? It would seem she and he would have to hold a serious discussion about respecting family boundaries. Later. When they were alone.

Clapping a hand on Nate's shoulder, he forced himself to relax. "C'mon, sport. Let's go see what's up."

With Nate beside him, he traveled the circular walkway around the house to the gate leading into the yard. As the cooking aromas intensified, his stomach growled, raising his ire several degrees. Hunger warred with pride, which waged a simultaneous battle with logic. Pulling the cord that lifted the latch, he opened the six-foot stockade gate. Once at the edge of the backyard, he stopped to stare at the domestic scene spread out before him.

Dad, dressed in jeans and a T-shirt, stood at the gas barbecue grill in a circle of smoke, fussing with a London broil and a rack of hot dogs. The meat hissed and sizzled over the flames while Dad swigged from a can of diet soda.

On the slab of cement that served as a basketball court, Scott dribbled past Brandy, who played point guard. The dog barked. Scott faked left, and then swooped the bright orange ball at the backboard. *Ka-thunk.* The ball hit the rim and slipped through the net. His back still to the newcomers, Scott shot up his arms and mimicked the reaction of the elated crowd in a hushed *"Rawwwwwwr!"*

In the opposite corner of the yard, far from where Scott practiced for his future with the New York Knicks, Summer sat upon a red and black fringed blanket under a pink dogwood tree in full bloom. Behind her, a wall of honeysuckle added bright green leaves and golden trumpet flowers like a halo around her head. Her floral-print skirt spread across her thighs and knees, creating a flat garden scene on his lawn. An artist could have painted her as the season she was named for right now.

Beside her, Maddie stood in a white sundress and matching sandals, waiting, hands on her skinny hips. "More!" she demanded.

Summer shook her head. "Not until you ask me nicely."

"More, please?" Maddie amended.

On a nod of satisfaction, Summer lifted a tiny plastic wand, pursed her lips, and blew a chain of bubbles that floated into the softening dusk. His laughing daughter, alert and apparently well healed from her foot injury, chased the fragile orbs, clapping her hands to pop them one by one.

Suddenly, a rogue firefly illuminated neon green near Maddie's head.

"Lightning bugs," she shouted, and took off after the insect, hands now cupped to capture a bit of nature's seasonal light.

The smile on his daughter's face eliminated the last vestiges of anger in Craig's gut, at least temporarily. If he'd held a camera right now, he would have snapped a photo to hold on to this image for the rest of his life. Despite his resentment at Summer's preparing this evening's entertainment, he couldn't argue with the results. They all looked so happy, so relaxed. So much happier than they would have been with pizza delivery or Chinese takeout.

While the weight of the world eased from his shoulders, he stepped deeper into the backyard.

Dad spotted them first. "Hey, guys! How'd the game go?"

"We lost," Nate said as he raced toward Scott and the basketball court. "Dude. Toss that ball my way."

"Change out of your cleats first," Craig scolded.

With a grin, Nate sat on the grass, untied the laces, and removed the cleats. Leaving them at the edge of the basketball court, he shot up and raced forward to play against his twin in his royal blue baseball socks.

Dad snorted. "I can see he's all choked up about losing the game."

"Yeah." Craig headed for the back door to the attached garage. To hold off the darkness settling around them, he flipped the switch on the outside lights. A growing colony of fireflies flitted around the yard, doing their best to attract their mates and keep the night at bay. "They got creamed, twelve to nothing. At the end of the game, the only one upset over the score was the coach. Maybe a few of the parents. Once the ice cream truck showed up in the parking lot, the kids couldn't have cared less about baseball." He nodded at the grill. "You need help?"

"Nah. Everything's under control. Have a seat, grab a beer."

"Soda's fine." He strode to the patio furniture and ducked under the canvas umbrella, where lit white mini-lights entwined around the stand and spines. He picked up a two-liter bottle and poured some chilled cola into a large red plastic cup. "You know you're not supposed to be eating beef."

"It's not beef," his father replied, focus still on the cooking meat. "It's a marinated turkey London broil."

"Turkey?"

"Summer picked it up. Along with some heart-healthy side dishes. She claims I won't notice the difference between tonight's meal and standard beef and potato salad."

Yeah, sure. And the moon was made of Swiss cheese.

Beverage in hand, Craig strolled over to the barbecue grill, tipped the cup to his lips, and murmured only loud enough for his father to hear. "Why didn't you stop her from insisting on this?"

"Stop her?" Dad replied in the same soft tone. "The barbecue was my idea."

Caught in midsip, Craig sputtered. "Yours?"

"Yeah. It's the least I could do after last night's calamity."

"Dad, we've been through that already. It was a mistake." He glanced at Maddie still chasing bubbles and bugs. "And judging by Maddie's hot pursuit, I'd say she's completely over last night's calamity."

"Well, I'm not," Dad grumbled. "And judging by the rings under your eyes, you're not either. So since Summer was headed to the supermarket anyway, I added a few things to her list, and together we whipped up tonight's dinner." He pushed the hot dogs with a long-handled fork, rolling them over to cook evenly. "Speaking of whipped up, wait'll you see the kitchen. She's got it completely organized and looking like something out of a catalog already. Summer's gonna be a big help to us, trust me."

Craig arched a brow. "*Et tu, Brute?*"

Dad smirked. "I know, I know. I wasn't wild about this whole Rainey-Day-Wife idea. But I've been doing some investigating online. The owner . . . April? I'm guessing she's related to Summer?"

"Her sister."

"Yeah, well, she seems to have a good head on her shoulders. Lots of testimonials from happy clients. And then I spent the last several hours talking to Summer." He pointed the fork in Summer's direction. "*She's* good people."

Good people. Highest praise from Dad.

Chapter Nine

"Wow." After two helpings of the teriyaki-marinated turkey London broil, apple fennel slaw, and garlic and herb roasted red potatoes, Craig had still managed to polish off a huge dish of blueberry cobbler that Summer had prepared for dessert. "I gotta hand it to you, Summer. That was amazing."

Summer shook her head. "Thank your dad. He did all the cooking. I just shopped."

"Don't fall for it, Craig. I only grilled the meat. She did the bulk of the work." Dad hoisted his can of diet soda in a salute. "I have to admit, when you promised me a heart-healthy meal, I pictured twigs and cardboard. But you made a fan out of me. Kids, what'd you think of tonight's dinner?"

"Awesome," Scott said.

"Yeah," Nate agreed.

And Maddie added her own "Yummy."

Dad chugged more soda, then announced, "I hereby cede the Hartmann family kitchen to your culinary expertise. From now on, you're in charge of dinner."

The kids actually applauded. Craig might have been insulted, but his brain couldn't argue with his stomach. She'd made a really great meal—a *healthy* meal—that even his picky eaters had devoured.

"Well, thank you very much, gentlemen." She turned to Madison. "And ladies."

When she smiled, Craig felt that familiar punch in the rib cage. He stumbled slightly as he rose from the bench at the picnic table, his empty plate in hand. "And to thank you for this magnificent feast, I'm going to clean up."

"No you won't." On the opposite side of the table, Summer got to her feet. "I'll handle this. It's getting late. Why don't you put your kids to bed and relax? You've got to be up early tomorrow."

He glanced at his watch and froze. Nearly ten o'clock? Where had the time gone tonight? He had to leave for work in six hours. His brain reviewed his return home from Nate's game, everyone so happy in the yard, the dinner, the easy banter between Summer and his dad. Once they'd finished the meal, they'd organized a Wiffle ball game with the kids until dessert time. And surprise, surprise. Summer was actually a heckuva Wiffle ball player.

Thanks to the power of suggestion, he yawned. God, he was beat. Summer's offer tempted him too much to resist. With last night's emergency-room dash followed by today's usual sporting-event runaround for the kids, he was already surviving on fumes. If he allowed Summer to handle cleanup, he could spend a few more minutes with his family before he collapsed into bed.

As if she understood his thought process, she shooed him with a hand. "Go. Scoot. The clock's ticking."

He reached for Maddie's plate, but Summer's next command stopped him. "Leave that. Your dad will help me clean up. Won't you, Ken?"

"Absolutely." Dad reached across the table and picked up the different jars of condiments, setting them on a large round platter. "Summer's right. As usual." He hauled her up against his side and wrapped an arm around her waist. "She's not only beautiful, she's smart, and she can cook. Someone oughta marry this girl, Craig. If you won't, I will."

Beautiful, smart, and a great cook. He certainly couldn't argue with any of those qualities. And Craig would add fun, generous, and forgiving. What kind of man walked away from such a perfect wife? He thought back to his telephone conversation with Brad on that fateful day. Even then he'd

suspected Summer's ex-husband was an idiot. Now he knew
for sure. No man in his right mind would let a woman like
Summer go. If she'd been *his* wife—

His brain screeched to a halt. She wasn't his wife; she was
his employee. The sooner he remembered to only think of
her in that capacity, the better for all of them.

Summer finally sank into bed in her new beige cave with her
Egyptian cotton sheets sometime after midnight. Exactly
what kind of appeal did brown have to the Hartmann men?
Every room in the house and all the furnishings seemed to
be decorated in some form of beige, cream, ecru, taupe, or
coffee. She couldn't wait to get to her storage facility and
pull out a few of her old wall hangings—anything to add a
splash of color. For heaven's sake, army barracks had more
style.

At least she'd managed to clean and organize the kitchen
this afternoon. Tomorrow she'd get the boys off to their day
camp after a healthy breakfast, then spend some time with
Maddie, find out how far behind she was for preschool. They'd
already begun covering manners today. Unfortunately, in
that area, the little girl had a lot to learn. She hoped the
child's ABCs hadn't been as badly neglected.

She reached to turn off the light when her cell phone, beside her on the nightstand, lit up and danced across the
surface. Who on earth . . . ?

Caller ID displayed Doug Sawyer's name and phone number. Now, what would Lyn's sweetie want at this time of
night? Panic slammed her chest. Oh, God. Lyn. Had something happened to her little sister? An accident?

She swung upright. Bare feet hitting the floor, ready to
flee at the mention of any drama, she punched the connect
button. "Doug. What's wrong? Where's Lyn?"

"Shoot. It's really late there, isn't it?"

His lazy West Virginia drawl registered on her panic. *If
this was an emergency, the alert you just heard would have*

been followed by frantic details. Her nerves calmed, and her heartbeat slowed to a more normal rhythm.

"I'm sorry, Summer," he continued in his country boy twang. "I had no idea it was past midnight by you. Lyn's fine. Do you want me to call you back tomorrow?"

She tried to bite back frustration, but failed miserably. "Like I'm going to be able to sleep now? Spill, Doug. What's wrong?"

"Nothing's wrong. Really. Go back to sleep. I'll call you tomorrow."

"You hang up now, and I'll drive to your place and gnaw off your left arm," she growled.

"You could try, but I'm in San Francisco for a story right now."

Doug, a reporter for *The Sportsman* monthly magazine, had lost his right arm while covering a story in Iraq. He and Lyn met while he participated in a rehabilitation program for amputees in Vermont, where he'd originally attempted to write a piece about the once-famous ski champ Brooklyn Raine. Instead, he'd fallen for her. They'd both fallen hard, judging by the goo-goo eyes they flashed at each other when they thought no one watched. Lyn and Doug had been nearly inseparable for the eighteen months that followed.

"I can wait until you get back to New York," Summer threatened. "And at that point, I'll start with your fingernails and work my way up very slowly. All they'll find when I'm done with you is some bleached-out bones."

"Wow. You Raine ladies sure are bloodthirsty."

She snorted. "Have you met our mom?"

"Yeah." He lowered his voice to a whisper. "She's scary."

Laughter spilled from her lips. "You didn't live with her, pal." With her pulse now normal and her curiosity piqued, she fluffed the pillows behind her and sat against the headboard. "So, what's up? Why the midnight phone call?"

His deep inhale whooshed through her phone's earpiece. "Okay, so I already asked April, and she said it's okay with her if it's okay with you. I know it's kind of unusual, but, I don't know. With you three, it just feels right, you know?"

And someone paid him to write for a living? Summer needed a GPS to follow this conversation. "Doug, I've spent the better part of the day with children. I have very few brain cells firing at one hundred percent right now. Think you can speak coherently before I slip into a coma?"

"Okay, here goes." He paused until the silence crawled under Summer's skin.

"Come *ooooonnnn,* Doug. I'm dying here."

"I want to ask Lyn to marry me."

"Really?" Exhaustion evaporated, chased away by excitement. Summer sat up even higher, clutched the blankets in her fist to keep from bouncing on the bed. "Ohmigod, that's awesome!"

"Yeah, well, hang on to that thought. Because I want to ask her at the rehearsal dinner next Saturday."

"Perfect."

"Ya think so?"

Joy infused her. "Yes, I think so. She'll be surrounded by family, at a celebration of love. I can't think of a better time for you to pop the question. April's good with it?"

"She's nearly as enthused as you are."

Summer grabbed her handy steno pad and pen from the nightstand and flipped to a clean page. "What do you need from me?"

"Aside from your okay? Nothing."

Her eyes nearly rolled into the back of her skull. *Deliver me from pigheaded men.* "Forgive me, Doug, but you know sports. You know nothing about romance."

"I know your sister."

"Not good enough. Her first husband proposed to her in Disney World on the Matterhorn in front of thousands of screaming fans. That's a tough one to top." Lyn and her fiancé, Marc Cheviot, had been world-class champions and the "snow bunnies" of alpine skiing at the time.

"Who said I wanted to top Cheviot's proposal?"

"Trust me, you want to top Cheviot's proposal. In a completely different, more adult fashion."

"And how exactly do you expect me to do that?"

"That's why you need my help. Give me a few days. I'll come up with something."

"No, you won't. I've got it all under control, Summer. This is one time you're not pulling the strings."

"But it has to be perfect," she argued.

"It will be. On my terms. And Lyn's. You've got enough to keep you busy. Play puppet master with April's wedding and the new job. How's it going, by the way?"

Surprise jolted her like a sudden clap of thunder in a quiet room. "How'd you know about my new job?"

"The Raine Grapevine. How else? April told Lyn. Lyn told me. So? Tell me about your first day. You survived, obviously. You okay?"

"I will be. The kids are adorable, if a little rough around the edges."

"Kids are supposed to be rough around the edges."

"Says the man with so much experience," she remarked dryly.

"Says my mom," he replied. "And she was a junior high school English teacher. She's got more experience with kids than me. Or you, if memory serves."

As the sarcasm volleyed between them, she marveled at her friendship with this man who would soon be her new brother-in-law. In the four or five years Lyn had been married to Marc, Summer had never felt comfortable enough to share a joke, a secret, a bit of snark with him. But Doug? Doug fit the family dynamic so well. Everyone liked him.

Well, except for Mom. *Gandhi* would have come to blows with Mom. And while Doug was no Gandhi, he was already family. The marriage proposal would make him more so.

Especially since she had no intention of letting him muck it up. Whether he wanted her help or not, she'd be there to make sure every detail was planned to perfection for Lyn.

Chapter Ten

When Craig entered the radio station on Monday morning, Maureen looked up from the pile of newspapers on her desk and grinned knowingly. "Wow. You look more relaxed today than you have in months."

"Yeah, amazing what a good night's uninterrupted sleep can do for a man." Still, he needed a cup of strong coffee to bring Cliff Hanger, manic morning man, to the forefront. Since Dad's heart attack, he only kept decaf in the house.

"So I take it your new 'wife' "—she curled her fingers into quotation marks—"is working out, huh?"

"She's not my wife. She's my employee." Words that had become his new catchphrase, which he repeated until he fell asleep, while he showered and shaved, and on the drive to work. At least, with all that practice, it rolled off his tongue fairly smoothly. He strode past Maureen and into the kitchen area where the commercial coffeemaker sat, prepared to dole out its usual sludge.

"Uh-oh."

To his dismay, Maureen had followed him, and now stood in the doorway, a sly look on her round face.

"Uh-oh what?"

She pointed an accusatory finger at him. The enormous butterfly ring that reached to her knuckle glinted in the overhead florescent light. "You like her."

He focused on the station's call letters in royal blue script emblazoned on the white ceramic mug in his hand. "Of course

I like her. You think I'd leave my kids with someone I despised?"

"No. Not you, Craig. You're Superdad. But there's a huge gap between despising someone and liking them. So tell me about the new woman in your life. What's she like?"

"How would I know?" He poured coffee into the mug, inhaled the nutty smell to stimulate his brain. "She's been in the house less than a day."

"Uh-huh."

After working with him all these years, Maureen knew him far too well. He wouldn't look at her, wouldn't give her an opportunity to see anything in his expression, real or imagined. Gathering a fistful of sugar packets, he turned and headed for his side of the studio for a little alone time prior to the start of today's shift.

Her last volley followed him down the hall to the overhead ON AIR light, which, thankfully, was not currently lit. "It's no great crime to admit you like a woman, Cliff."

"When I find one I like, I'll let you know, sweetheart." On that note, he opened the studio door.

Jerry Patton, overnight deejay, looked up from the cart machine and nodded. "Hey, Cliff. Welcome back." He reached across to shake Craig's hand. "How's it going? How's your dad?"

"Pretty good. How's everything here?"

"Not bad. Line two is iffy today, keeps cutting out. I already told Lenny."

"Great, thanks."

As if their discussion conjured him up, Lenny chimed in over the loudspeaker. "Cliff? You got a personal call on line one."

Panic slammed his chest. First day back and five minutes in there's a problem. As he reached for the receiver, Jerry backed away and quietly slipped out of the studio.

Alone, Craig punched the blinking light on the phone. "Hello?"

"Craig? It's Chelsea."

Like he'd forgotten the sound of his ex-wife's voice. "Chelsea?" He glanced at the clock overhead. 5:45 in the morning. At least, for *him*. "Where are you calling from?"

"London," she replied.

That explained the early-morning phone call, since London was about five hours ahead, as well as the slight British edge to her speech. Chelsea had a habit of absorbing accents wherever she went.

"London. Wow. How're you doing?"

"*We're* fine. How are you? I see you've gone back to work. Do you think it's wise leaving our children in your father's care all day, what with his condition and all?"

In other words, she was still asking for an excuse to seize custody. Good thing she didn't know about Maddie's trip to the emergency room the other night. "The children are fine, and so is Dad, thanks for asking." Sarcasm sharpened his tone to a razor's edge.

On a deep breath, he recalled Summer sitting on the blanket in the grass last night, lips pursed as she blew bubbles for Maddie to chase. The laughter, the relaxed atmosphere, the delicious and healthy food, and his first decent night's sleep in God knew how long. All thanks to Summer.

"Trust me, Chelsea. We're all in perfect hands right now."

Monday morning's alarm clock buzzed at precisely six o'clock. Summer hit the floor with her usual high energy, schedule running through her head as well as scrawled in her notepad. Doug's news last night went a long way toward giving her a happy outlook on the coming week. And plans. She had more plans to make that would provide Lyn with the romantic moment she deserved. First, however, she had to see to her new charges.

After a quick workout with her DVD program, she prepared a cup of coffee and some fruit for breakfast. Showered, dressed, and hair styled, she descended the staircase to the first floor and knocked on the twins' bedroom door at exactly seven thirty. "Let's go, boys. Time to get ready for camp."

In the kitchen, she found all the morning materials the same way she'd left them the night before. Place settings sat on the dinette table: cereal bowls, spoons, napkins, and tumblers. Backpacks stuffed with bathing suits, sunscreen, towels, and a change of clothes rested on the clean floor against the wall. Opening the refrigerator, she pulled out the lunches she'd made, then placed them into the individually labeled, insulated bags for each boy. Sandwiches, drinks, fresh peaches for dessert, and because she didn't want their little bodies to go into total shock, a few Oreos. Each completed lunch bag found its way into the corresponding backpack.

By the time the boys stumbled to their chairs, she had cereal with fresh strawberries in their bowls, milk ready to pour, and orange juice in the glass tumblers for them.

Nate looked down at the bowl, then up to give her the stink eye. "We usually just have juice and a Pop-Tart."

"New person in charge, new rules," she replied. "Besides, your bodies will go farther on better fuel."

"Like a car on premium gas?" Scott asked.

"Yeah, sure. Why not?"

"Except most cars don't need premium gas," Nate replied, still studying his breakfast with the reticence normally reserved for a nuclear power plant. "It's a rip-off to get people to pay more at the pump. The only cars that need premium gas are sports cars and stuff. Ferraris, Porsches, BMWs."

This kid probably had a promising future as a defense attorney. "So, if you were a car, which would you rather be, Nate? A Ferrari or an old jalopy?"

"Neither. I'd be a Porsche Carrera. That car can go from zero to sixty in four and a half seconds. *Vroom! Vroom!*" He held his arms out straight, hands cupped slightly, pretending to grip a steering wheel.

"You think the Porsche does that on regular gas?"

"No."

"You've just made my point." Summer pointed to the bowls. "Now eat, both of you."

As she turned her back on them, Nate's loud whisper still reached her ears. "Dude. I think she's serious."

"Well, then," Ken said from the doorway, "you better listen to her."

Summer turned toward where he stood, scruffy and sleep-worn in another pajama-top-and-sweatpants combination, with his granddaughter clad in her nightgown riding one hip. "Good morning."

"Good morning, Summer." He bounced Maddie. "Say good morning, sweetheart."

"Good morning, sweetheart," the little girl parroted.

Summer laughed. "How long did that little comedy routine take you?"

"About ten minutes," Ken admitted with a grin, then turned to the two children seated at the table. "I think it's safe to say, boys, that Summer's not going to fall for any of your antics the way I used to. Better dig in to that breakfast or she's liable to give you kippers and eggs tomorrow."

"What's kippers?" Scott asked.

With a wink at Ken, Summer leaned close and declared, "Really stinky fish."

A child's chorus of "Eeeeeewwww!" broke out around the adults. A moment later, the music of spoons hitting cereal bowls resonated through the kitchen.

"Well played, Summer," Ken said with a chuckle as he strode to Maddie's booster seat. "This little one can have the same breakfast as her brothers, minus the strawberries."

"Already got it." Thank God the paperwork Craig had filed included Maddie's allergy.

"When I eat strawbabies, I get pink and itchy," Maddie chirped.

"I know," Summer replied as she placed the bowl of plain cereal in front of the little girl. "Your daddy told me."

"What else did Daddy tell you?"

"What did he say about *us?*" Scott pressed.

Oh, no. Not again. "Eat." She pointed at all three bowls. "You boys have a bus to catch. And Miss Maddie and I have an appointment with Dr. Seuss."

"Who's Dr. Zoos?" Maddie asked.

"He's not a real doctor, you know," Nate said.

"Yes," Summer replied. "Thank you for clearing that up." She turned to Maddie. "Dr. Seuss writes storybooks."

"I used to like *One Fish Two Fish Red Fish Blue Fish* when I was little," Scott said. "But you should probably read *Fox in Socks* to Maddie."

"Don't fall for it, Summer," Ken said. "These imps recommended *Fox in Socks* when I read to Maddie last week. I nearly fractured my tongue getting all the rhymes out. The boys just want to amuse themselves at your expense."

The snorts and giggles erupting from the male end of the table confirmed their guilt. Before she could offer them more than a scalding glare, a *honk-honk* outside signaled the arrival of the camp bus.

With a screech of chairs on tile and the thump of backpacks, the twins raced out of the kitchen. "Bye, Gramps. See you later."

Summer watched from the window as they climbed aboard the yellow school bus. The doors closed behind them, the red lights stopped flashing, and the bus pulled away from the curb.

In their wake, the boys had left behind a puddle of orange juice, spilled sugar, and bowls clogged with soggy cereal floating in lakes of milk. No farewell for Summer. Not even a "thanks for breakfast" had passed their lips.

I love a challenge, she reminded herself for at least the hundredth time since yesterday.

With breakfast done and the kitchen clean once again, Summer planned to get Maddie dressed after Ken left for his appointment at cardiac rehab. As she lifted the little girl from her seat at the table, Ken called to her from the front room.

"I took Maddie's booster seat out of my car in case you have to run any errands before I get back. Do you need me to set it up for you?"

"No, I'll be fine," she replied. Honestly. How hard could it be to put a car seat into a car?

"All right then. I'll be home in a few hours."

"Take your time." She bounced Maddie on her hip. "Okay, princess. Let's get you dressed."

"Minidress," Maddie chirped as Summer carried her down the hall. "I want my minidress."

"Sounds good to me. Minidress it is." She opened the door to Maddie's room and stifled a gasp.

No brown in here. Maddie's room was pink from carpet to walls to linens. The bed, dresser, and nightstands were French provincial. Their white and gold lines broke up the mass of pink like an aspirin floating in an ocean of Pepto-Bismol.

She bent to set Maddie on the floor, and swallowed her distaste. "What a pretty room you have!" Kinda like the inside of a Barbie box.

Giggling, Maddie raced to the closet. "Minidress." On tiptoe, she reached the knob and pulled open the door.

Apparently, the Pepto obsession didn't end in the bedroom. Most of the dresses hanging from the low rail inside the closet were in some shade of pink, as if the men in this household would somehow forget Maddie was a girl unless she was surrounded by the most feminine of colors.

"Minidress, minidress," Maddie sang over and over. "Minidress, minidress."

Summer strolled to the closet and pulled out a pink dress with ladybugs embroidered along the hem. "How's this one?"

"No. I want my minidress."

"Okay." Which one was the minidress? She opted for another sundress, this one candy-striped pink and white. "This one?"

Maddie shook her head vigorously. "No. My minidress!"

Again, Summer studied the closet's contents. Mini equaled

short. What was the shortest dress in there? She found a tunic-style top with floral leggings. "Let's try this one."

"No, no, no!" Maddie screeched. Face red, hands fisted, and feet stomping the floor, Maddie provided Summer with her first view of what she'd heard referred to as "conniption."

Thanks to the training she'd gone through with Rainey-Day-Wife, Summer knew what to do.

"All right then." She had to shout to be heard over the child's angry screams. "I suppose you don't want to get dressed after all. I'll just leave until you've calmed down."

She turned and left the room, but lingered in the hall outside the door. A minute passed where the noise from the bedroom grew louder, then Maddie began to gag. Oh God, was she going to puke now? Surrendering, she turned to re-enter the room. She hadn't taken more than two steps when the choking and the screaming stopped simultaneously. No doubt, the gagging had actually appeased the tantrum, and Maddie calmed down on her own. Summer stopped, waiting for the next turn of events.

At last, the fit of temper and threat of vomit abated on several snorts. Seconds later, Maddie poked her head outside her room, her elfin face awash in tears. "I want my minidress."

Summer folder her arms over her chest. "Well, Miss Maddie, a temper tantrum is not a good way to get what you want. So once you've calmed down enough, you'll tell me you're sorry and we can begin again."

The child had the grace to drop her gaze to her feet. "Sorry."

Not the most sincere apology, but it was a start. Summer sighed her defeat. "Okay. Now, since I obviously don't know which dress you want, will you please show me?"

Maddie's mood went from thunderstorm to sunshine, and she beamed. "Minidress!"

"Yes, yes, I know. Show me."

With Summer behind her, Maddie skipped to the closet and, arm extended upward, pointed to the shelf above her head. Bouncing, she continued her song. "Minidress, mini-dress, minidress . . ."

Ah. Among the stack of books, hats, mittens, and scarves on the overhead shelf sat a folded square of red and white polka-dot fabric. The moment Summer pulled the dress from the shelf, she realized her mistake.

Not a minidress. A *Minnie* dress. The ten-inch image of Minnie Mouse's grinning face sewn to the bodice made the child's demands clear. The fabric was abrasive, some kind of polyester mix that wouldn't breathe and would no doubt wilt any female past puberty. Due in part to the stiff tulle that flared out the skirt, the garment was also pretty heavy.

Summer frowned. "Are you sure you want to wear this?" She didn't add *in this heat?* but the words floated between the two of them.

Maddie's bouncing became a joyful dance while the song remained the same. "Minnie dress, Minnie dress, Minnie dress."

Time to concede the battle, if only to halt that particular phrase from filling the air all day. Too much more, and the other adults would come home later to find Summer banging her head against the wall and repeating *Minnie dress, Minnie dress* in some kind of psychotic breakdown. "Okay. One Minnie dress coming up."

Chapter Eleven

To Summer's surprise—and relief—Maddie wasn't behind in her education at all. In fact, academically, she was probably ahead of most four-year-olds, with a complete grasp of the alphabet, numbers to one hundred, and a keen sense of who should win the next presidential election. Yes, Grandpa had covered all the important bases.

Socially, on the other hand, the little girl would definitely benefit from some interaction with other children in her age group. Concepts such as sharing, *please* and *thank you,* picking up after herself, and gracefully accepting the word *no* escaped her child's mind. A drawback for the lone little girl in a household of men. Maddie, treated like a princess, ruled the Hartmann homestead with the severity of a tyrant. Summer realized she had an uphill battle with this little girl. She'd have to address her concerns with Craig, though—see how far he'd allow her to discipline Maddie.

While they sat together in the living room reading *The Cat in the Hat* for the umpteenth time, Summer's cell phone jangled. The caller ID image displayed FLOWERS BY MONET.

"Excuse me a sec, sweetie." Extricating herself from Maddie and the sunken couch, she answered on the second ring. "Hello?"

"Summer? It's Elsa. How are you today?"

"Fine, thanks. What's up?"

"I wanted to let you know. Those new roses we talked about? They're in."

"They are? Oh, that's great." More than great. Phenomenal.

Stupendous. April would be thrilled. But the first law of business was never let the seller see your excitement.

"I was hoping you and April would have time to stop by and see them this afternoon."

Frowning, she cast a glance at Maddie still cuddled up with Dr. Seuss. "Today?" Tiny Terror in a flower shop? She shivered at the imagined destruction. At least with April there, though, she'd have reinforcements. April had *lots* of experience with troubled children.

"If you can, yes," Elsa replied. "I know it's last-minute, but I'll need extra time to order from the wholesaler. Every day counts. That is, of course, if you want them."

Roses with blooms shaped like hearts? Oh, she wanted them, all right. Based only on the photos Elsa had shown her last week. She took a deep breath to calm the adrenaline racing through her bloodstream. "Let me check with April and see when she's available. I'll call you right back."

"Okay, but don't wait too long—"

"I understand," Summer interjected. "As soon as I hear from April, I'll be in touch. Thanks, Elsa."

Before the floral designer could argue, Summer disconnected the call, then punched in April's number. As she waited for her sister to answer, she picked up a few of the tiny cars that littered the floor like a salvage yard.

One ring, a yellow Mustang. Two rings, a lime green Corvette. Three rings, a red pickup. At last, on the fourth ring, with a bright blue PT Cruiser in her palm, April answered. She barely got the word *hello* out before Summer jumped in.

"How soon can you get to Monet?"

A pause. An orange VW Beetle.

"The florist?" April finally asked.

"Yes, the florist. Elsa just called me. The heart roses came in, and we're getting first look."

"Oh my God. Really?" Excitement crackled like static between them. "How soon can *you* get there?"

After setting the collection of cars into the open carrying case on the floor, she gazed at the booster seat in the corner of the room. "I'll have to bring Maddie, but we can be there in about a half hour."

"You're on! I'll see you there." She took a deep breath, exhaled, then added sotto voce, "How's everything going over there?"

Summer stole another glance at Maddie, smiling and tapping the toes of her black patent leather shoes to some unheard song. "Okay. A lot to do, but that's a good thing, right?"

"Just remember I'm a phone call away if you need me."

Summer turned and tiptoed into the kitchen, lowering her voice to a whisper. "Actually, there *is* something you can help me with. Rainey-Day-Wife has preschool referrals, right?"

April's reply was a guarded "Yes."

"I want to set up some appointments for Craig and Maddie to check out a few."

"Isn't it a little too soon to start phasing yourself out? You've only been there a day."

Did April really think she planned to turn tail and run already? "No, sister dear. I'm not that flighty. Maddie needs the social interaction. She's sweet and smart as a whip, but a little spoiled."

"Ah. Okay. Got it. In that case, I'll have Bonnie make a few phone calls and print off a list of possibilities. Anything else?"

"Nope. Just get to the florist ASAP."

"Honey, I'm in there like swimwear." She hung up before Summer inhaled the next breath.

Stuffing the cell in her pocket, Summer returned to the living room, where Maddie still sat, clicking her toes. "Want to go see some really pretty flowers?"

The child looked up from her book and shrugged. "Okay."

"Good. I have to strap your booster seat in my car. While I'm doing that, put your book on the shelf and pick up some of your Barbies."

Maddie's expression darkened, and she tossed the book on the floor. "I don't wanna."

"It's important that we pick up after ourselves, Maddie."

Folding her arms over her chest, she stuck out her lower lip. "Why?"

"Because if we all left our belongings wherever we choose, the house would be cluttered and people could get hurt."

"Grampa left some staples in my room. I got hurt."

"Well, then, there you are. You've just made my point. So you put away the book and pick up your dolls while I get us ready to go to the flower shop."

She shook her head. "No."

Oh, great. She *so* did not have time for a diva scene right now. And if Maddie dug in her heels, what could she do? She couldn't exactly leave the kid here alone.

But did Maddie know that?

With no other options, she'd have to roll those dice. "Okay, then. You'll have to stay here by yourself until I get back. Be sure you lock the door behind me."

When Maddie didn't move off the couch, Summer upped the ante and strode toward the stairs to fetch her purse from her apartment. "See you later."

"No! No! No!" Maddie shouted loud enough to rattle the windows. Ear-piercing shrieks followed, along with the now-familiar gagging.

This time, Summer didn't rush to the child's aid. On the landing between the two floors, she peeked around the corner and frowned at the little girl stomping her feet. "Not another temper tantrum, Maddie," she remarked with a stern look.

Maddie stilled instantly, one foot raised in midstomp. Slowly, she dropped the foot to the floor and shook her head, eyes downcast.

"Do you want to come with me or not?"

Sniff. "Yes."

"Then you know what you have to do."

Her head dipped lower, and she murmured in a barely audible voice, "Sorry."

"That's better." A little more sincere this time. Progress. "Thank you, Maddie."

The child actually bent to pick up one of the naked dolls.

Looking up, eyes swimming, she asked, "Will you wait for me, please?"

Summer smiled. "Of course."

When Craig opened the front door in the early afternoon, Brandy, on a series of *woof*s, charged across the tiled floor and launched herself at him.

"Down, girl." Her black nose swiped moisture across his cheek. "Brandy, get down." He gently pushed the dog away. Too late. Long golden hairs clung to his jeans and shirt. Stupid dog. Why hadn't he convinced the kids to adopt a Chihuahua? Or even better, a goldfish?

"Hello? Anyone home?" He hung his keys on the hook near the door and stood, waiting for some kind of human reply. Nothing.

Gut churning, he remembered the last time he'd come home to an empty house. The day Chelsea walked out. She'd left a note in the kitchen, telling him she couldn't live with him anymore and that she'd taken the kids to a hotel to consider her next move. *Her* next move. Like he didn't have a say in the demise of their marriage.

His heart thudded in his chest as he approached the immaculate kitchen. Chelsea was currently in London, wasn't she? Or did she only say she was an ocean away to throw him off? To lull him into a false sense of security, so she could swoop in and take the kids away from him while he sat blissfully unaware at work?

No. She wouldn't dare, not so long as her new husband, Jake McIntyre, had his eye on becoming a real estate tycoon to rival Donald Trump. In Jake's eyes, bad publicity was worse than no publicity.

Besides, if she'd shown up here, demanding her kids, surely Summer would have called him. Right? She wouldn't just hand Maddie over to a stranger and leave. Would she? There had to be a reasonable explanation why no one was here.

Yeah, sure. Like Dad had another heart attack, and Summer

left in such a rush to get to the hospital, she forgot to call him. Or there was an accident at camp with one of the boys.

Or she was really a plant hired by Chelsea to kidnap the kids. First day—*bam!* They're hiding out in some other town with new identities so he could never find them.

Maureen had done a news story on that a few years ago. Some guy had hired a close friend to kidnap his ten-year-old daughter from a playground and hide her in a motel in another town until the cops had verified the dad's alibi. Once the authorities and ex-wife focused their attention on a stranger abduction, Dad retrieved his daughter from the kidnapper, and they hightailed it to New Zealand.

New Zealand.

The little girl's mom, who had full legal custody, wound up paying a fortune to private investigators, then fighting through international lawyers for years to get her only daughter back. By the time the kid came home, she was enrolled in college. Within a year, as an adult, she moved back to New Zealand, leaving the mom alone once again.

Back in the day, Cliff Hanger had spent over an hour coming up with humorous commentary about that poor mother's situation. He remembered quips regarding boomerangs and kangaroo pockets specifically. Funny stuff at the time. Now? Not so funny after all.

Calm down, idiot. Summer doesn't even know Chelsea. Think of reasonable explanations. We're out of milk. Or Maddie's foot got infected from chasing lightning bugs last night, and they went to the pediatrician. Or the boys forgot their lunches, and Summer and Maddie drove to the camp to drop off a few sandwiches.

The sound of a car door slamming outside broke the stillness. Craig rushed to the front door in time to spot Maddie leaping out of Summer's Escalade. She wore a beaming smile, a wreath of roses around her head, and her Minnie Mouse costume. As she skipped beside Summer, her little mouth moved rapidly. At this distance, he couldn't hear what she chattered about, but her happiness registered clearly.

Panic ebbed, freeing the constriction in his chest, before annoyance set in. He yanked open the front door and stood waiting on the top step.

"Daddy!" Breaking away from Summer, Maddie raced to him. A dozen strips of red and white ribbons attached to the wreath streamed behind her like a vapor trail. When she reached him, she wrapped her arms around his waist.

Tension seeped out of him in a steady stream. "Hey, sweetheart. Don't you look pretty?"

She glanced up at him. "Uh-huh. Summer let me wear my Minnie dress."

A choice he definitely planned to address with Summer when they were alone. But for now, he just smiled. "I see that. Where'd you get the flowers?"

"April Showers brought me flowers," she replied on a giggle, then dropped her hold on him and headed for the door. "Gotta go potty."

Well accustomed to the brief window of time between that statement and an accident, he whipped the door open for her. "By all means. Go."

She dashed off at the same time Summer reached the porch. "Close. My sister, April *Raine,* gave her the wreath, not April Showers." Hitching her purse higher on her shoulder, she flashed him a smile that could melt Antarctica. "Hi."

"Hi," he said, then steeled himself for a confrontation. "Got a minute?"

"Sure. What's up?"

He frowned. "First off, why is my daughter dressed in her Halloween costume?"

A rosy blush flamed her cheeks, and she spluttered, "That was totally my fault. A breakdown in communication. By the time I realized what she meant by minidress—"

"In other words, she hustled you."

"Yeah, I guess so." She laughed, light and joyful. "I promise it won't happen again."

When was the last time he laughed like that? He pushed the thought from his mind and focused on the emotions that had churned through his gut when he'd first come home. "More importantly, where did you take my daughter without telling me?"

She flinched as if he'd raised a hand to her. A moment later, her expression hardened to steel. "I didn't exactly run away with her."

"I know that," he retorted. While he kept his gaze level with her face, his feet shuffled slightly. Yeah, okay. He sounded like a lunatic. A pretty common occurrence whenever he was around her. Which was stupid, considering he'd made a name for himself as a talk show host. "I just would have liked some advance notice that I'd be coming home to an empty house."

No reaction, not even a blink. "The empty house isn't totally my doing. Your dad went for cardiac rehab this morning and called a while ago to say he'd stopped at the VFW to spend time with the guys. And in case you've forgotten, your sons will be home from camp in about fifteen minutes. That should pretty much cover any concerns you have."

Not quite. He folded his arms over his chest. "And you and Maddie?"

"Something came up that couldn't wait, and I had to run out. What did you expect me to do? Leave Maddie home alone for an hour or two?"

"Of course not. But you really shouldn't be driving Maddie around without her car seat."

Summer's expression turned stony. "Out of curiosity, Craig, did you happen to read any of the paperwork you signed at Rainey-Day-Wife? Because I can assure you, my sister doesn't hire idiots to work for her. The safety of the children we care for is always our main priority. Your father left me the booster seat in case I needed it. And son of a gun, I did. I'm sorry I didn't write you a note telling you where we'd gone, but by the time I got Maddie to pick up her toys, I was already late for my appointment."

Dragging Maddie into the argument? Low blow. "So it's my daughter's fault?"

Summer threw up her hands in a gesture of surrender. "Oh, for God's sake. It's no one's fault. Nothing happened. Maddie and I ran a quick errand. No accidents, no tragedies, everyone's safe. If the worst that happened is you didn't have your fan club waiting at the door when you came home from work, I don't see the reason for an inquisition."

"I—"

She didn't give him a chance to finish. "How about I wait while you fetch a rubber hose to beat a confession out of me? You know what? Forget it. Don't bother. I'll tell all. I took your daughter to the florist for an hour or so. We looked at flowers. She got a wreath for her hair. Happy now?"

Yes and no. He'd insulted her, and he owed her an apology. But the passion in her tone impressed the heck out of him. "I'm sor—"

"Save it." She shot up a hand in front of his face. "I've got things to do, and you're holding me up. Unless I'm fired?"

What were the chances she wouldn't cut him off a third time? Unwilling to roll those dice, he simply shook his head.

"No? Good." She strode past him, her annoyance a heat wave that blasted his face. "By the way, my sister gave me a list of preschool options for Maddie. After dinner, I'd like to go over them with you."

She didn't even hold the door for him. Instead, she stormed inside. By the time he picked up his jaw and followed her, she'd disappeared up the stairs. Her ire told him one thing for sure.

Chelsea wouldn't stand a chance against Summer Raine.

And for that reason alone, relief flooded him from head to toe.

Chapter Twelve

At the end of the first week, Summer felt pretty darned proud of herself. By now, the morning routine went off without a hitch, thanks to her night-before prep. The boys ate their breakfast, minus the commentary. No "thank you" when they raced out the door for the bus yet, but they actually said good-bye to her now. Maddie, although still prone to tantrums, charmed her with funny smiles, crayon drawings, and dandelion bouquets. Small steps, she reminded herself.

Ken seemed completely at ease with her presence in the household, often sitting in the kitchen with her, helping while she cooked dinner or washed dishes. On Wednesday, he had pulled out an old family photo album and shared pictures of Craig as a boy. An adorable, clumsy, moody boy with braces, long hair, and a scowl that never really masked the humor in his vivid eyes.

Of all the Hartmanns, however, Craig, the man, puzzled Summer most. Their conversations were generally easy banter, until she attempted to discuss the children. Then he became visibly rigid. Like when she showed him the list of preschools from April. He'd immediately stiffened up, took the paper from her, folded it, and stuffed it in his pocket. She found it on Thursday when she did the laundry. Still in his pocket. Didn't he realize how important it was for him to get Maddie used to social situations? Well, she'd have to keep poking—gently, but consistently.

I love a challenge.

Since Craig had a staff meeting Friday afternoon, Summer

was in charge of getting both boys to their baseball games after camp. Two cases of water bottles, two minicoolers, and two gear bags later, she gathered all three children into her Escalade with ten minutes to spare. At least today both boys were at the same park, same field. Their teams were playing against each other.

Once at the field, she unloaded the boys with their gear, then removed Maddie from her booster seat and grabbed the tote bag full of "busy stuff" she'd amassed to keep the little girl from becoming bored. God, she hoped she hadn't forgotten anything.

With a deep breath, she took Maddie by one hand and slung the tote over her shoulder. Once they crossed the parking lot, she scanned the half dozen baseball diamonds for the familiar uniform colors worn by the twins. Of course, she finally spotted them in Field Six, the farthest corner of the park. Another inhale and she continued the schlep across what felt like a quarter mile of grass.

"Summer?" Maddie chirped. "Can I go on the slide?"

Oh, thank God. A full square of playground equipment stood a few feet away from the boys' baseball field. A slide, several swings, a balance beam, and cartoon animals on giant springs would keep Maddie active and entertained. The spongy alphabet blocks that served as flooring underneath the equipment would keep her safe from injury. Easy decision, for once.

"Go for it, sweetheart."

On a screech, Maddie released her hand and took off toward the slide. With the little girl distracted, Summer settled on the middle tier of the bleachers, where she could see all three Hartmann children clearly.

Bug spray. The thing she forgot? Bug spray. No matter where Summer sat, the mosquitoes found her. After fifteen minutes perched above the high damp grass, her ankles were ringed in itchy welts. An hour later, the pesky bugs had moved up her calves and across her bare arms.

Meanwhile, the sun continued to broil, reflecting off the

metal bench and baking her skin clay-dry. *Bug spray and moisturizer would have been nice today.*

"Well, hi there," a female voice with a very Southern twang said.

Summer turned to find a curvaceous woman seated beside her. She wore a clingy black T-shirt and jeans so tight her leg veins were probably strangled. Her round face, beneath a mop of overprocessed blond hair, split into a wide grin.

"I haven't seen you here before," she continued. "I'm Karen Miller, team mom for the Nino's Pizza team."

"My name's Summer." This time she opted to skip her last name, avoid the cutesy reaction. "I'm here with the Hart-mann boys."

"Oh." Karen scanned the baseball players, then returned her gaze to Summer. "How's their grandfather doing?"

"Fine, I guess. I mean, he looks okay. He's not happy about drinking decaf, but . . ." She let the statement trail off. What else could she say, having only met this woman a mere minute ago?

"And Craig?" Karen's heavily made-up eyes studied the parents seated in the bleachers. "Is he here?"

"Still at work. He should be here in a little while."

Karen shook her head. "Poor Craig. He's had a rough time, what with his dad's heart problems. But I guess you already know that." Her eyes narrowed in scrutiny. "Are *you* family?"

"No." She sensed Karen wanted more detail, but she didn't feel the need to divulge. Instead, she turned her attention to the baseball game.

The boy at the plate swung at a perfect curveball and sent it into foul territory, where the first baseman bobbled the catch.

Karen clucked her tongue. "My son would have caught that easily."

Summer stared at the woman, slack-jawed. Gee, that was rude. "Which boy is your son?"

She pointed to a child leaning against the fence that

delineated the visiting team's dugout. "That's Jason. He's been benched for two games because he had the nerve to call attention to a teammate's incompetence during last week's game." Her tone grew bitter and biting. "Apparently, Coach Dave believes it's more important to protect a kid's feelings than to teach a winning spirit."

As Karen ranted about the injustice dealt to her son, Summer didn't know who she pitied more: Coach Dave or the perfect Jason. Clearly, the boy learned his lack of sportsmanship from his mother.

The next batter struck out, and Karen muttered, "Oh, for God's sake. Jason would have crushed that last pitch."

From the haze of her memory, an image popped into Summer's head. April, several years ago, near tears as she talked about a similar experience. Her son, Michael, on a little league team, was taunted by the coach's son, a bully who delighted in poking fun at a child with Down syndrome. At the time, Summer hadn't understood why April simply didn't put her son in a league with other handicapped children.

"Why would I do that? To make the bully more comfortable? Mike's an excellent player, and more importantly, a good kid. He deserves *all* the opportunities in life. And I'll do everything in my power to make sure he gets them."

Holy crow, how many ignoramuses had April fought with to make good on that vow? And here, Summer thought April had only found her backbone after she met Jeff. Ha. What a moron Summer was. April had always had the fight in her—she just saved her energies for the important battles, rather than the petty ones.

At that moment, Scott stepped up to the plate, and Summer focused all her attention on him. First pitch he slammed into the hole near second base. The ball bounced into the outfield, and Scott legged a double easily. Caught up in the moment, Summer cheered, "Way to go, Scott! *Woot, woot!*"

"I don't suppose Craig told you that today was Scott's turn for the oranges and snacks?" Karen's question stopped Summer in midwhoop.

"Huh?"

Karen sighed. "I figured as much. Each week, I've assigned one child's parents to bring sliced oranges for the kids to eat during the seventh-inning stretch and snacks for after the game. Today was Scott's turn."

"Oh. I . . . ummm . . . I didn't know." She looked past the field at the crowded parking lot. "Is there a supermarket around here somewhere?" Maybe she could pick up the items when Craig got here.

On an overly dramatic sigh, Karen flitted her fingers in Summer's face. "Forget it. That's part of being a team mom, anticipating when someone might drop the ball. I've got extra oranges and snacks in my car. But next week Nate will have to bring them. Would you tell Craig for me?"

Around them, the crowd erupted in a roar. The batter after Scott hit a screamer that sailed way out into center field. Scott took off for third. Nate, on the opposing team, caught the ball and fired it to the third baseman. Scott collided hard with the other boy. Both fell to the dirt. The third baseman got up.

Scott didn't.

Craig raced into the emergency room, his heart pounding a frantic tattoo against his chest. He came to a halt at the reception desk and grabbed the edge as if to keep from falling. "I'm Craig Hartmann. My son Scott came in here a little while ago?"

The nurse behind the desk scanned her computer. "He's in Exam Room Five, through that door, down the hall, to the left." She pointed past the waiting room, where dozens of people in varying degrees of suffering sat in plastic orange chairs. "I'll buzz you through."

He turned, and the antiseptic smell nearly knocked him to his knees. God, he hated hospitals. Exhaling, he strode past the guard, heard the buzz, and pushed through the double doors. On shaky legs, he bypassed the first few curtained areas until he found the one beneath the number five. Pushing the

sickly green cloth barrier aside, he came face to face with
Scott. The boy reclined in a hospital bed, his left leg elevated
and wearing an ice wrap. Beside the bed stood Nate on the
right, and Summer seated in a chair on the left with a sleepy-
eyed Maddie in her lap.

"Hey, Dad," Scott said at the same time Summer greeted
him with, "Craig. It's okay. He's going to be okay."

He swallowed hard, allowed himself a few seconds to ab-
sorb Summer's reassurance. His skeleton sagged with relief.
"It's okay?"

"The doctor thinks it's either a sprain or a small fracture
to the growth plate. We're waiting for the X-rays. He'll need
to see an orthopedist, and his baseball career is over for this
season, but he's going to be okay."

"I'm getting a cast, Dad," Scott exclaimed. "Isn't that awesome?"

"Awesome," he replied blandly.

Maddie yawned, and Craig turned back to Summer. "Why
don't you take the other kids home? I think they've had
enough excitement for one night."

"Not yet," Nate said. "Summer promised us something from
the hospital cafeteria."

His lips quirked, and one eyebrow arched. "You're kidding."

She shrugged. "Apparently, that's awesome too."

"Oh, I'll bet."

"It's probably going to be a while before we hear from the
doctors," she said as she slowly rose, still holding Maddie.
"You sure you don't want me to stick around?"

"No. You look drained, and Maddie's clearly wiped. Go
home. Feed the kids and put them to bed. I'll bring this guy
home as soon as he's fixed up."

She nodded. "I'll bring you a coffee before I leave."

"From the cafeteria?" He bugged out his eyes with exag-
gerated excitement. "Awesome."

The warmth of her soft laughter lingered long after she'd
taken the kids from the ward. Alone with Scott, he pulled up

the chair next to the bed and sat, cupping his son's hand. "So tell me, sport. How'd you manage this?"

Scott grinned. "It was awesome, Dad. Third inning, we're down by one, and I hit a double . . ."

When Craig finally carried Scott inside the house sometime around eleven P.M., Summer was waiting. She shot up from the living room couch, and the magazine she'd been reading fell to the floor.

"How is he?" she whispered as she bent to pick up the glossy tabloid.

"Zonked out on painkillers, his knee in a cast, but flush with his 'awesome' adventure. He fractured the growth plate. Not bad, but bad enough to sideline him for a few weeks. Your job here seems to be getting exponentially harder rather than easier." He glanced around. "Where's everybody else?"

"Sleeping. Including your father, who thought he could overrule me. I assured him Scott was okay, just a little banged up, and he'd see for himself in the morning." After placing the magazine on the side table, she tiptoed closer. "And how are *you?*"

He laughed bitterly. "Getting far too familiar with the inner workings of the emergency room." With his arms tingling from lack of circulation, he shifted Scott, and the boy sighed in his sleep.

Summer slipped her arms under Scott's sleeping body, brushing against Craig's bare forearms. "Here. Let me take him. You should go to bed."

"That's okay, I've got him." He pulled his son closer, which pulled Summer closer. Her face was a breath from his.

The only light in the room, a pale glow from the lamp on the side table, illuminated her high cheekbones and lush lips. The air stilled, and Craig couldn't catch his breath. He struggled to tear his gaze away from her mouth, those moist, parted lips, the shallow inhale and exhale. Leaning closer, she tilted her head slightly. He stretched toward her, dying to taste her.

"Mommy?"

Scott's soft plea broke the spell. Craig snapped back as if on a bungee cord.

"No, honey, it's Summer," she murmured. "Go back to sleep." Scooping the boy against her chest, she told Craig, "Go to bed. You've got work in the morning."

As she carried her burden down the hall, Craig could only stand in the dim living room, slack-jawed. He'd almost kissed her. If Scott hadn't called out . . .

He shook off the haze. She's an employee, he reminded himself. *She's just an employee.* To avoid running into her on her way out of Scott's and Nate's bedroom, he locked himself in the half-bath adjacent to the front door. No way he'd fall asleep now. Summer's image would remain in his mind all night. And he could do without dreams that involved kissing her. With the cold tap running full blast, he splashed his face with icy water.

Sleep was overrated anyway.

Chapter Thirteen

Just when Summer had created a comfortable routine with Maddie, Scott's injury threw a greased monkey wrench into the works. Once Nate left for camp on Monday morning, she set Scott up in the living room, where he'd have access to television and videos and remain in Summer's earshot at all times. Maddie, however, unaccustomed to sharing the television, her grandfather, or even Summer's attention during the day, threw tantrums over the smallest incidents.

On Monday, when Scott wouldn't change the channel, she threw a Barbie at him. On Tuesday, she pitched a fit because Summer wouldn't let her eat her lunch on a tray in the living room like Scott. She tossed her spaghetti onto the kitchen floor, then dumped her chocolate milk on top of the pasta mess.

On Wednesday, she kicked Scott's injured leg because he wouldn't get off her side of the couch. At that point, Summer sent the little tyrant to her room for the rest of the day. Enough was enough. This child needed to learn to get along with others.

When Craig finally arrived home that afternoon, she waited for him on the porch, a familiar folded piece of paper in her fist. "Would you care to explain why I found this in with your dirty laundry?"

He stood on the step below her, studying the paper as if seeing it for the first time. "Sure. If you tell me what it is first."

"It's the list April compiled. The list of preschools for Maddie."

"So that's where that went." He grabbed the paper from her, opened the front door, and stepped inside. "Sorry. I must have forgotten to take it out of my pocket. I'll start making calls tomorrow." He strode away from her, dismissing her concerns, and headed toward the living room. "Hey, kids! Daddy's home."

She stayed right on his heels. "I'm not done with you. I'd like to talk to you about this."

"Can it wait? Nate has football practice."

"Nate has football practice in two hours," she snapped. "He's prepped and ready to go, right down to his cleats and mouthpiece in his gear bag. Since I give you all of my time whenever you need it, I think you can reciprocate by giving me a few minutes when I ask."

He stopped, blinked, then slowly exhaled a breath. "O-kay . . . Give me twenty minutes or so first? Please?"

"Fine. Meet me in my apartment. I don't want the children to overhear our discussion." As if to emphasize her mood, she stomped up the staircase with enough drama to out-diva Maddie.

Once in her shabby little kitchen, Summer couldn't stop shaking. In thirty-five years, no one had ever prodded her into a full-blown hissy fit. Until now. While Maddie's bad behavior played a role, a deeper current threatened her sense of balance. Craig unnerved her, a fact that didn't sit well in her normally placid head.

Funny. She'd survived her mother's strident demands in her childhood, sailed through the mean girl years of junior high and high school, and currently ran interference for the media event of the season, all without breaking a sweat. Even Brad had never cracked her perfect veneer. The night she'd tossed him out of the house, she'd been vindictive, but calm. She'd never raised her voice, never really lost her composure. Not like she had with Craig.

Barely two weeks into her position here, she'd become a virago, a shrieking siren of outrage. *Not good, Sum. Not good at all.*

She pulled out her trusty pad to write a new list. This one would detail all the issues she wanted to discuss with Craig. Without a list, Craig Hartmann could wreak havoc with her concentration. The man had a habit of making her palms sweat, kicking up her heartbeat, and stealing her ability to think straight.

Well, not today. She had things to say—important things. She refused to allow his bright blue eyes and boyish charm to distract her. And that scruff on his face . . . mmm. Rugged and so appealing.

Stop. Focus, Summer.

For the next few minutes, she repeated the list over and over, committing the details to memory. Unfortunately, a rhythmic knock on her door sent all her practiced lines flying like dandelion fluff in the wind. She opened the door to find him holding a fistful of pink roses, daisies, and orange tiger lilies. Her steely composure melted.

"I come in peace," he said as he thrust the cellophane-wrapped bouquet toward her.

She took the flowers and offered a shaky "Th-thank you." On closer inspection, she noticed the yellow grocery tag stuck to the cellophane. The fireworks inside her head ka-boomed to a crescendo. How sweet. When he'd asked for time, she thought he was stalling. Apparently, he wanted the extra minutes to create this surprise for her.

She quirked a smile. Who would have thought she'd appreciate a seven-dollar bouquet from the local convenience store? The woman who had always insisted on the very best? Sometimes, though, the very best had more to do with simplicity than shine.

She stole a glance at Craig over the crinkly-clear flower wrapper. The man didn't have an ounce of sophistication. Her ex-husband had the sheen of New York success: the right clothes, the right hair, the right car. At face value, to most people, Craig couldn't compare to Brad. Craig wore his hair a little too long, and his jeans and T-shirt always lent him a slightly rumpled appearance. Yet Craig was ten times the man Brad could ever be. Because Craig had integrity, honesty, and the right set of values.

While she headed to the tiny kitchen for a makeshift vase, he stepped inside the apartment but loitered near the door. "I owe you an apology."

Pulling a long-necked water pitcher from her cabinet, she looked up and managed a tremulous smile. "Good. That makes us even, since I owe you one too."

"You?" He shook his head. "No. I'm the villain here. I've been miserable to you, and you've been terrific."

The smile lighting up his features hit her square in the heart. *Focus, Summer.* She turned on the tap and placed the pitcher beneath the running faucet. "I berated you like a judge passing sentence on a convicted felon."

"You wanna talk felon? I practically accused you of kidnapping my daughter last week. I think my crimes have been a lot worse."

Well, she really couldn't argue with that. "Okay, you win." With a paring knife, while holding each individual flower under the running water, she clipped a bit off the stem at an angle. Then she arranged the blooms one by one in the canteen. When she had the arrangement adjusted perfectly, she set the bouquet on the counter between her and Craig—an effective barrier to keep her sane. "Apology accepted."

"Good." He moved to the side, rendering her wall useless in two easy steps. His eyes danced with delightful sparks like shooting stars. "So what did you want to talk to me about?"

What *had* she wanted to talk about? Something about his kids, right? Frantic, she sought out the yellow legal pad she'd left in plain sight on the counter. The bold words on top of her list screamed at her. *Don't let him distract you!* Yeah, sure. Easy to write when she was alone. Not so easy to heed when he was inches away from her suddenly flushed face and flip-flopping heart. She glanced at the list again.

Number one. Maddie's behavior. Be nice, but firm.

"Umm . . . I wanted to talk about your children. Umm . . . about what exactly I can and cannot do with them."

He quirked a brow.

Okay, that sounded totally creepy. "Discipline-wise, I mean."

The light fled from his eyes, and deep lines etched his forehead. "Did you have some kind of problem today?"

Today? How about every day? Recalling Madison's tantrums, she found her mettle. "As a matter of fact, yes. You do realize your daughter's a brat, right?" *Oh, God.* She slapped a hand over her mouth, a minute too late.

Craig stiffened, eyes narrowed to slits. "Really?"

Wow. Way to go, Summer. You managed to be firm without being nice. She blew out a breath to release the tension. Unsuccessfully. The air crackled with resentment. "I'm sorry. I shouldn't have said that."

"But you did."

"Yeah, I did," she admitted. *In a moment of profound idiocy.* "And I guess, well, to be honest, I meant it."

"You *meant* it," he repeated with a frown. "Do tell."

She winced at the ice in his tone. Fisting her hands, she held her ground. Maybe blunt was best when dealing with this issue. With this man. "Craig, I'm sorry. Honestly. But you must have seen the tantrums Maddie throws when she doesn't get her way."

He waved her off. "All kids throw tantrums."

"Maddie screams herself sick—literally. She nearly vomits when she gets riled up."

"Oh, come on." He snorted. "You're making that up."

"No, I'm not."

"Well, what did she want?"

"What doesn't she want?" she retorted. "She started her demands the very first day with her Minnie dress. Since then, we've battled about picking up her toys, why she can't eat in the living room, and how much television time she can have. Today, she kicked Scott in the knee. The *injured* knee. All because he wouldn't move out of her spot on the couch."

"I can't believe she went that ballistic over something so simple. What else did she want?"

"Nothing. Apparently, she thinks if she creates a big enough drama, she'll get her way." She stared hard at Craig.

In response, he picked up an errant daisy petal and flipped it between his fingers. "Yeah, I guess Dad and I are a little softer with Maddie than we are with the boys."

On a sigh, Summer leaned forward and folded her hands on the counter. "Then you're doing her and yourselves a huge disfavor."

He crushed the petal in his fist. "She's four, for God's sake. Her mother walked out before she was six months old."

"She doesn't need excuses for her bad behavior, Craig. She needs the social interaction and structure of preschool. She needs boundaries."

His head snapped up, ire suffusing his face bright red. "Don't tell me. Let me guess. You want to erect those boundaries."

"No. I want to help *you* erect those boundaries. You're her father. But I need boundaries as well. I need to know how you expect me to discipline all three of your children, but especially Maddie. I'm with her most of the day. 'Wait till your father gets home' isn't an effective deterrent to bad behavior, particularly if Dad has a tradition of being too soft on her."

"How have you handled the tantrums so far?"

"When she blows her stack, I usually leave the room."

His mouth gaped. "Even though she's making herself sick?"

"No, you misunderstand. I step out of her sight, but I'm never more than ten feet away from her, in case she needs me. I only let her see I'm there after she calms down."

"And does she always calm down?"

"Yes."

"On her own."

"More or less, yes."

"So? Looks like you've got your answer. Just keep doing that."

She sighed. "That's a temporary fix, and it won't work for

every issue, particularly if the rest of the family continues to give in to her demands."

"Why?" His glare hardened. "Have you caught her playing with matches? Or juggling meat cleavers?"

"No, of course not."

"Then leave her alone. You're making a big deal out of nothing."

He couldn't be that naive. "It's not *nothing.*"

"Yeah, it is."

"Craig, the boundaries you set now are vital to her well-being."

He slapped the petal palm-down on the counter and raked a hand through his hair. "Jeez, what a day. First, Chelsea calls me for my weekly reminder that I'm a lousy father. Now you're going to back up her accusations because my four-year-old didn't want to pick up her toys."

"She kicked Scott!" Summer took a deep breath, blew it out, then inhaled and exhaled again. Calmer now, she cupped his fingers in her palm. "I'm not saying you're a lousy father. But you have to provide her with a strong sense of what's right and wrong now. That way, she'll be prepared to make smart choices for the rest of her life."

He yanked his hand out of her grasp and pushed out of reach. "Look, just forget it. Leave Maddie's discipline to me. I'll talk to her."

"She's four. You can't just talk to her."

"She's my daughter. I'll talk to her." He turned and strode from the apartment, leaving her door wide open. His heavy thuds as he descended the stairs echoed every beat of her heart.

Chapter Fourteen

The following morning, after a miserable night spent tossing and turning, Craig still stewed about his conversation with Summer.

Maddie was a brat.

Deep in his gut, Craig had always suspected he and Dad spoiled her rotten. But to have Summer come right out and say it? Ouch, that stung. When he sat at the controls in the studio during morning drive time, he blurted out the question before thinking. "Do you think children need boundaries, Maureen?"

His sidekick, ensconced in her booth across from him, stared as if he'd lost his mind.

"Don't give me that bug-eyed look," he scolded with his usual Cliff Hanger sarcasm. "I'm serious. A friend and I were discussing this yesterday. Now, everyone knows I have no use for parenting advice. That's the beauty of remaining blissfully unattached. But yesterday, I heard about a kid who throws tantrums where she screams and cries so much she practically pukes. Charming, right?"

"Cliff." Maureen's tone held a tentative warning, the kind she'd offer a friend who stood on the edge of a frozen lake on a warm spring day. "Are you sure you want to go there?"

"Absolutely. Call it idle curiosity. Let's hear from some parents out there. Is this kid's behavior normal? And how would *you* deal with a spoiled brat? Time out? Take something away from her? Lock her in her room until she's thirty?

Or do you just give in to make the screaming stop? What do *you* say, Maureen?"

"I think most child psychologists advise parents to ignore temper tantrums, unless there's a danger the kid will hurt himself. And even then, you should remove the danger but not indulge the tantrum."

"So . . . what? Like if the kid's holding an AK-47, you rush him and take it away? And hope he doesn't plug you full of holes first?"

"No, stupid," she retorted for the audience's delight. But the grin she flashed held no malice in their usual on-air rapport. "Like . . ." She paused, then shook her head. "I don't know. My son was never a tantrum thrower, thank God."

"Wait, what are you telling us? You think your kid's perfect? 'Cuz lemme tell ya something, Maureen. I've met your son."

"I *know* Blake's no angel, Cliff. He just never resorted to tantrums to get his way. I sometimes wish he had, because it probably would have been a lot safer."

"Yeah? Why? What'd he do?"

"Blake was always a go-getter. Tell him no, he'd go get whatever he wanted himself."

Leaning closer to the mike, he flashed a thumbs-up. "Like what? Come on, Maureen, give us details."

She paused for a heartbeat. "Like when he first learned how to get out of his crib at night. Most kids climb over the rail to escape, but not my little Houdini. He'd take the crib apart."

"You're kidding."

She laughed. "I wish. He never cried or screamed to get out. But every night, I'd put him in, and a few hours later he'd pop up next to my bed. He'd figured out how to unscrew the foot of the crib from the rail. Didn't matter how tight my husband made those screws. That boy got 'em apart night after night for weeks. I was terrified he'd swallow one."

"So how'd you stop him?"

"We broke down and bought him a toddler bed. And not

once did he ever climb out or take it apart. I guess by eliminating the danger, we eliminated the challenge, so he stopped leaving his bed at night."

He pointed a finger at her, pistol-style. "That's why you're part of my team, Maureen. You're my voice of reason. I probably would have tied the kid to the crib."

Summer awoke to Craig's voice in her bedroom. "So how would you handle a brat?"

"Huh?" She jerked upright, sheet clutched to the neckline of her nightshirt, expecting to see him in the doorway. Finding herself alone, she exhaled relief.

Craig's intrusion sounded once again, breaking the gray silence of dawn. "So far, the callers seem to agree with Maureen and my friend at home that kids need boundaries."

She glanced at her bedside table. The radio! Craig was on the air.

No. *Cliff Hanger* was on the air. Discussing whether or not children needed boundaries.

Anger roused her from the bed, and she slammed a palm on the clock radio to turn off the voice in her room. Of all the idiotic stunts. Oh, just wait till he got home this afternoon. She'd blast him good. What kind of insensitive clod aired a private conversation to the delight of a national audience?

Later, she promised herself. Right now, she had a family to care for. Later, she and he would have yet another heart-to-heart, this time regarding what was off-limits to his radio audience.

She hadn't signed up for this kind of notoriety. He'd already humiliated her on the air once, and she'd forgiven him. And okay, he was ticked off that she'd called Maddie a brat. He'd made that clear with his stormy departure last night. Still . . .

That didn't give him the right to hold her up to public ridicule. Again.

After breakfast, with Nate off to camp and the rest of the family in the living room, she washed the dishes and cleaned the kitchen. Her fury at Craig, however, needed a stronger outlet, something she could destroy or beat. Something on which she could take out her frustration with a little harmless violence.

"Hey, Maddie?" She approached the little girl, who was watching an educational television program in the den with her brother and grandfather. "Wanna play outside for a while?"

Maddie shrugged and scooted forward. "Okay."

Perfect.

Ken tilted his head to one side. "You okay, kiddo?"

"Yeah, I'm fine." She turned toward the window, refusing to let him get a closer look at her face. "It's so nice out. I thought I'd take a whack at the weeds around the house. You wouldn't happen to have any gardening supplies, would you?"

"Sure." He rose stiffly. "In the garage. I'll show you." He turned to the children. "Stay put, guys. We'll be right back." Still wearing his slippers, he shuffled to the utility room, then led her into the two-car garage, where he flipped on the light.

To Summer's amazement, this was the one area of the house well-organized and well-provisioned. An assortment of tools hung on pegboards on the walls. Lawn-care items, including a ride-on mower, took up one corner. Among the outdoor maintenance equipment, a workout bench and treadmill reigned incongruous but supreme. On a shelf near the door, she found a tub of pastel-colored chalk, which gave her a wonderful idea for Maddie.

"Here you go." Ken lifted a plastic ten-gallon pail. "There's shears, trowels, gloves, probably even a hat in this thing." He ducked his head. "This was Chelsea's stuff. I don't think Craig's touched any of it since . . . you know."

Yeah, she knew. Since the divorce. Thinking back to her destructive night with Brad's personal items, she winced. Go figure. Craig had a more generous spirit than she did. Then she remembered this morning's radio show. Anger spiked anew.

With the bucket of chalk in one hand, the pail of gardening tools in the other, she murmured a quick thanks before returning to the living room. "Come on, Maddie. Let's go catch some rays."

"Are those like lightning bugs?"

Scott clucked his tongue. "She means sunshine, dummy."

Summer cast a harsh glance at him. "Scott. Not nice."

"Sorry," he murmured.

"Come on, sweetheart." She held out her hand toward Maddie. "We'll need a little sunscreen, and you should put on shoes, because while I do some gardening, I thought you might like to play hopscotch. Do you know how to play hopscotch?"

"Nuh-uh."

As she'd suspected. Another drawback to growing up in a male-dominated household. "That's okay. I'm going to teach you. It's a lot of fun. My sisters and I used to play all day long."

Until Brooklyn showed such proficiency in skiing when she was eight. Then it became April and Summer on the hopscotch grid. Where April always tore her shorts, skinned her knees, lost buttons, and generally bore the brunt of Mom's resentment at their father's absence. Summer sighed. Poor April. She hadn't exactly taken the easy road in life. At least now she finally knew happiness.

"Summer?" Maddie's tug on her skirt shook her back to the present.

"Right. Sorry. Let's get you dressed and ready."

Maddie skipped down the hall, a familiar chant filling the air. "Minnie dress, Minnie dress."

Oh, no. Not again. "*No* Minnie dress today."

The child whirled, her little face screwed up like dried fruit.

One quick, warning "Maddie . . ." halted the tantrum before it gathered steam. The child's face smoothed, and though her lip puckered in a pout, no protest filled the air.

Satisfied, Summer smiled. "Good girl."

I love a challenge.

Craig pulled into the driveway in the early afternoon and marveled at the sense of peace that enveloped him. Just three and a half weeks ago, coming home meant racing around like a lunatic, corralling three kids for dinner and then whatever extracurricular activity was scheduled for that day.

Amazing. In less than a month's time, Summer had turned his chaotic existence into a more manageable family lifestyle. Even the house looked happier. Which was odd, really . . .

Stepping out of the van, he studied the front yard. The house definitely looked better. The windows sparkled in the afternoon sunlight. The flower beds held dark soil and no weeds. And the gutters. Someone had repaired the elbows at the top of the leaders. Who? When?

Dad. Had to be Dad. Craig's blood pressure soared. Did the old coot really want another extended stay at the hospital?

"Dad!" he shouted as he sped up the walkway toward the front door.

"He's with Maddie in the backyard." Summer's answer seemed to come from on high. "Nate and Scott are playing video games inside."

Craig scanned his surroundings, even peeked in the windows, without spotting her. Suddenly, everything clicked. He strode around to the side of the house, looking up toward the second story, and drew in a sharp breath. Summer perched at the top of his industrial ladder, at least twelve feet off the ground.

"What in God's name are you doing up there?" he growled.

"Cleaning out the gutters." She swiveled slightly, her right hand covered in a thick red rubber glove from fingertips to elbow, and held up a clump of wet black leaves and twigs. "They're so clogged with gunk, it's a wonder excess rain hasn't damaged your roof. Yet."

He glanced at the clump only briefly. From his angle on ground level, he had a fantastic view of her long legs and sassy curves, clad in pale yellow shorts. Above the shorts, a short-sleeve tailored shirt in a yellow and white checkered pattern tied at her waist left the barest wisp of flawless skin visible to the sun. And to him.

Despite the afternoon heat, a cold sweat broke out under his arms and on the back of his neck. *She's an employee.* And even if she wasn't, she didn't deserve to be ogled like a Playboy bunny. The ladder, propped on uneven ground, wobbled.

"Watch out!" He raced forward and steadied the two sides with his hands. Summer never reacted, just kept digging in the gutter. "Have you lost your mind?"

"No, I'm trying to save you a fortune in home improvement costs." The smile she flashed didn't mask the coolness in her eyes. "You're welcome."

Hostility? This early in the day? From a woman dangling two stories up? Okay, he'd been married long enough to recognize when a woman was ticked at him. And yeah, he kinda knew he owed her an apology for last night. He just didn't anticipate she'd hold a grudge. "Is this about last night? Would it help if I said I'm sorry? And that you were right?"

"Really?" She released the muddy clump, which fell toward him.

He took a step sideways while the clump landed in the lined garbage can a foot away from him. *Kathump.*

"Who told you?" Acid dripped from her words. "Your audience?"

Ah. Now the hostility made sense. A little. "You heard the broadcast?"

"Not the whole thing. Just enough to know that I was today's feature." She frowned, an angry angel on high. "Really, Craig. I thought I'd already done my time as entertainment on your show."

"I never mentioned your name, Summer. Nor did I say you're taking care of my kids, because, as far as my audience knows, I have no kids. Cliff Hanger's a single dude with no patience for children."

"Yeah, great. Keep hiding behind your carefully constructed façade, pal. But guess what? *Craig Hartmann* has three kids and has hired a woman to care for them. A woman who pretty much knows what she's doing. You might want to heed *her* advice, rather than polling the yahoos who call in to your show."

He spread his hands wide, forced his expression to newborn innocence. "Point taken. If you'd like to talk about this in detail, though, you'll have to come down here. I'm not much into the whole sermon-on-the-mount bit."

"Fine." She sent another muddy missile plummeting downward, then peeled off the gloves. "I have to drop off two of your screens at the home improvement store anyway. Might as well do it now."

"Great. I'll go with you. The van's still fairly cool, so I'll drive."

He swallowed hard when her bottom wiggled as she descended the ladder, rung by rung.

"That's not necessary."

"Of course it's necessary. And I'll pay you back for any money you've laid out for all you've done today. The house looks great, by the way. Thanks."

"I didn't lay out any money today." She landed beside him, a frown marring her pretty face. "I used all of your exwife's gardening stuff and, I'm assuming, your tools. And you're welcome. Now go spend some time with your family while I hit the store. Alone." She swiped an arm across her face, which did more harm than good.

"You can berate me all the way there and back," he offered, with a self-deprecating grin.

Dirt smudged her cheeks and forehead. Sweat dotted her upper lip and throat. And he still thought she looked prettier than a perfect sunset, all warm and vibrant. *Just an employee, just an employee . . .*

At last, she smiled—a real smile, not a Canal Street knockoff. "In that case, you've got yourself a deal." She pointed to two ripped screens leaning against the garage door. "Grab those, would you? I'm just going to let your father and Maddie know we're going." She strode toward the gate.

"You're not gonna change first?"

She craned her neck to reply, "No. What would be the point? I'm not done with the gutters. This is only a break so I can berate you, remember?"

"Right. Okay, then. Let's do it." After using his key fob to open the van's sliding door, he picked up the torn screens. Once he had them stowed in the back, he climbed into the driver's seat and started the engine. The air conditioning blasted his face, a bit warm at first but soon cooler.

A minute or two later, Summer traipsed the walkway, opened the passenger door, and climbed in. "Your daughter has demanded a surprise," she remarked. "Although, what she expects you to bring back from Hardware Expo, I can't begin to imagine."

"Tattoos," he replied.

She cast him a quizzical glance while buckling her seat belt. "Excuse me?"

"Temporary tattoos. From the gumball machine near the exit."

"Ah. Of course."

He sensed the unspoken criticism, *But she's not spoiled at all, Craig.* Unfortunately, no witty riposte came to mind, so he simply put the van in reverse and backed out of the driveway.

For several minutes, Summer stared out the passenger window, saying nothing.

Craig tensed, fingers gripping the steering wheel, white-knuckled. When he reached the highway without incident or commentary, he allowed himself to relax.

"Here's the thing," she announced suddenly.

He hit the brake so hard, she lurched forward. One hand shot out to catch the dashboard.

She stared at him agape. "Easy there, cowboy."

"Sorry," he murmured. "For a second, I lost the car in front of me in the sun."

"Uh-huh." Her dubious look made him squirm. "Anyway, I'm really not comfortable with the idea that our private conversations are aired for your public's consumption."

"I told you. No one knows who you are. Or that we were, in fact, discussing my daughter."

She shook her head. "That's not good enough. I want your

promise that nothing that goes on between us, whether it's a conversation, a meal, or a television show we watch, will be broadcast on the air."

Annoyance prickled the fine hairs on his nape. "Summer, I host a radio show. Do you have any idea how hard it is to fill four hours of airtime five days a week?"

"You play music as well. Not like talk radio hosts."

"Because I've already cut a significant chunk of my life away by refusing to talk about my personal life."

"In case you didn't notice, I'm part of your personal life."

"You're an employee." Oh, boy. That was *not* the right thing to say at this juncture.

For the briefest moment, hurt registered in her widened eyes, but with the flick of a stray bit of hair from her face, she pulled her emotions under control. "You're right," she said flatly. "I suppose that gives you the right to use me in any capacity that makes your life easier. By all means, then. Talk about me. You can even use my name. Who knows? Maybe in time, I'll be as famous as my sisters."

"That's not what I meant, Summer."

She waved off his apology. "That's quite all right, Mr. Hartmann."

"Craig," he corrected.

"No, Mr. Hartmann. You're my employer. It's inappropriate for me to use your first name."

"Oh, for God's sake, knock it off, Summer. We're friends, okay?"

"No. Apparently we're not."

Chapter Fifteen

Summer stared out the window and willed her body not to shake. *An employee.* Why did that sting so much? After all, this was a temporary job for her, not a lifetime career. So what if he saw her as Alice to his Mr. Brady—with or without the lovely ladies with hair of gold? She wanted this to remain a professional relationship, a job. Nothing more. Didn't she?

He'd barely pulled into the parking lot and put the van in park before she opened her door. "You don't have to come inside with me, Mr. Hartmann. I'll only be a few minutes."

Please let him stay in the car. She needed the space—the distraction—to keep her emotions in check. Before he slid the side door fully open, she reached in and grabbed the screens. "Be right back," she announced with forced cheer.

Head down, screens tucked under her arm, she stumbled toward the entrance. His footsteps sounded behind her, but she didn't stop.

"Summer, will you wait up, please?" he demanded.

"Summer?" The second male voice came from the double doors at the exit side of the large hardware warehouse. "It *is* you."

Oh, God, no. Not Brad. Not now, with nowhere to run, nowhere to hide. She turned slowly and faced her ex-husband with what she hoped came across as cool disdain. "Brad? What are you doing here?"

Brad, looking smug and superior as usual, wrapped an arm around the young, perky brunette glued to his hip and rubbed her rounded belly. "Briana and I are modeling the *nursery.*"

The blow hit Summer in the stomach and behind the knees simultaneously. "Congratulations," she managed to eke out before the buzz overwhelmed her brain. She felt herself collapsing, prepared to welcome the slam of the pavement.

"Whoa, easy there, Summer." Craig's firm grip on her elbow, and the support of his chest against her back, kept her upright. "I think you've had way too much sun for one day. When we get home, you're going to sit inside and rest. No argument." With one arm still supporting Summer around the waist, he thrust out a hand. "Craig Hartmann."

"Brad Jackson. And this is my wife, Briana."

"Nice to meet you both, but I better get Summer inside and cooled off." As he turned to hustle her away, Briana fired a parting shot.

"She didn't look like an ice princess to me, Brad. In fact, she looked kind of pathetic."

Craig stiffened. "Pathetic?"

"No, Craig." Summer placed a hand on his sleeve. "Don't. Just let it go."

"Not on a bet." He prodded her over to a nearby bench and propped the screens up against the handrail. "Sit. I've got this." Loud enough to stop traffic on the highway, he shouted after the departing couple. "You wanna know what's pathetic, sweetheart? Finding out your boyfriend's married by calling in to a radio show, breaking up his marriage, and then planning a future with the weasel."

Summer winced. "Craig, please." Her face burned with embarrassment. Several people, carts loaded with two-by-fours and plywood or bags of home goods, stopped to stare. Their gazes traveled from Craig to her, then to Brad and Briana beating a hasty retreat through the parking lot.

Craig turned back to her with a gratified smile. "All done." Picking up the screens, he jerked his head toward the entrance. "Come on, sunshine. Let's go get some screens fixed.

Play your cards right, I might take you out for dinner afterward."

"I can't go out for dinner." She rose, stretched her arms wide, and gestured at her stained shorts, the mud spattering her ankles, the red welts from bug bites on her legs. "Look at me."

"You look great."

Yeah, right. This was definitely not the pose she'd hoped to strike the first time she saw her ex-husband since their divorce was final. Why couldn't she have run into Brad next week at April's wedding? When she'd be wearing a couture gown and be totally in her element, running the social event of the year? But no. She had to come face-to-face with him and his child bride—who was already with child herself— when she was an emotional and physical wreck. "I look like I just crawled out of a swamp."

"Nah." He threw a casual arm around her shoulders. "Swamp creatures are usually green from all the algae. Besides, where I'm planning to take you, it won't matter."

"Yeah? Why's that? It's dark?"

"No." He led her inside, the screens gripped against his waist. "I think I'm going to keep it a surprise for now."

"Please, no. I've had enough surprises for one day."

He squeezed her harder against his side. "Trust me."

Trust him? Throwing his earlier words back at him, she mumbled, "Not on a bet."

With the screens dropped off for repair, Craig made a phone call to his father at home before leaving the Hardware Expo parking lot. "Order in takeout for you and the kids. Summer and I are going to be a little longer than I anticipated."

Summer swerved her gaze his way, disapproval etched on her face. "Craig!"

He cupped a hand over the mouthpiece. "Relax. The kids will enjoy a little junk food for a change. They've been eating healthy stuff since you arrived. Their poor bodies are going into withdrawal, what with all those leafy vegetables and juicy fruits." Dropping his hand again, he finished his conversation with his dad.

"Everything okay, Craig?" Dad asked.

"Yeah, we're fine. We just need to talk about some stuff, and I'd prefer to do it without an audience, if you catch my drift."

"Okay, then. I'll let the kids know. And Craig? Whatever Summer wants to talk about, you be sure to listen to her. She knows a lot and she only wants what's best for you and the kids. Ya hear?"

"I hear."

"She's good people."

He cast a sidelong glance her way. "Yeah, I've heard that before. Thanks, Dad. Bye." Flipping the phone closed, he turned to Summer. "Ready?"

She arched a brow. "For what?"

"Dinner, of course." He started the engine and put the van in drive.

On a sigh, she turned to stare out the window. "I guess so."

A wave of sympathy washed over him. Dealing with an ex was never easy. And from what he'd seen in today's exchange, Summer needed someone to talk to, someone who could make her see the humor in what happened. If there *was* any humor in what happened. "And we're off," he announced as he drove out of the parking lot.

Minutes later, he pulled into the drive-through line at a fast food joint.

That's when Summer finally turned to face him, her expression one of pure disgust. "You're kidding, right?"

"Nope. For what it's worth, this place offers a veggie burger combo. I've never eaten it, of course, but I've heard it's pretty tasty. As veggie burgers go, I suppose." He shrugged. "Me? I'm an all-beef-patty kinda guy. So what's it going to be?"

Another sigh. "I guess I'll have the veggie burger."

He slipped into a fake French accent. "An *excellent* choice, *mademoiselle.* Of course you'll want that with a side order of *pommes frites.* And may I suggest a bit of the bubbly to go with your meal? We have a wonderful California cola, or would you prefer the bouquet of the more citrusy lemon-lime soda to complement your dining experience?"

She finally cracked a smile—hesitant, but there nonetheless. "Oh, the lemon-lime, definitely. Diet."

"*Oui.* It will be as you wish, *mademoiselle.*" When they rolled up to the speaker, he placed their order, adding two apple pies. "For dessert," he told her with a wink.

At the window, the clerk handed out the soft drinks first, and he set them in the cupholder in the console. When he took the bag of food, he passed it to Summer. She started to open it, but he crushed the top of the bag in his fist. "Nope. Not yet. I'll tell you when."

After leaving the restaurant, he drove down the main road leading to the local beach. He pulled into the narrow strip of parking lot that faced the water and parked. He lifted the arm of his seat, grabbed the bag of food from Summer, and fumbled his way into the passenger section. Once he unclipped Maddie's booster seat, tossed it into the back of the van, and brushed the few stray Cheerios off the gray cloth of the seat, he signaled Summer to join him.

"Come on." He patted the seat, then pointed to the fiery sun sinking into the Long Island Sound. "Dinner and a show."

She settled beside him with a ghost of a smile.

"Here, have a French fry." He passed her the cardboard box of uniform deep-fried potatoes. "That should make you happy."

"Is that all it takes for you to be happy?"

Digging inside the bag, he located her veggie burger, held it out to her. "Sometimes, yeah. You wanna tell me what happened back there with your ex?"

She practically ripped the burger out of his hand. "Not particularly. You want to tell me about Chelsea?"

"Touché."

"I mean, I knew he married the twit," she blurted. "I just

didn't know the twit was with twitlet." She turned to stare out the passenger window and sighed heavily. "You have no idea how much that hurts."

Silence reigned for several long minutes as they ate.

"I have to tell you," Summer said at last. "This is not a very good veggie burger."

"It's from a fast food joint. What'd you expect?"

Her smile a tad more genuine, she nodded, bit into another French fry. "The fries are good though. It's been years since I had them."

He saluted her with his bacon cheeseburger. "Welcome to the dark side."

Finished with her sandwich, she crumpled the wrapper and dropped it into the bag. The sun had already sunk beneath the waterline of the Long Island Sound. Twilight settled around them.

"How about a walk?" he suggested. "Before security tosses us outta here?"

She shrugged. "I guess."

"Whoa, easy, Summer. That's way too much enthusiasm for a simple little walk on the beach on a nice summer evening. You might wanna rein in your excitement."

Another half-smile flashed on her face. "I guess I'm not very good company tonight."

"You had a bad day, and I'm sorry about that." He picked up the bag full of trash, stood slouched so as not to bang his head on the van's roof, and stepped carefully past Summer to open the sliding door. "Come on. It's a nice night."

Once on the pavement, he turned to help her step out.

"Thanks." She smoothed her shorts with her hands, which instantly had Craig appreciating her long legs yet again. "It's not your fault, you know." When he simply stared at her without replying, she added, "Okay, you weren't exactly blameless. And I was really peeved at you. Now I'm just mad at myself."

Tearing his gaze away from her legs, he closed the door and locked the van. "I've been there. But don't go kicking yourself. He's a bum, you're better off without him."

"Let's just take that walk and enjoy the evening, okay?"

In other words, he'd touched on a taboo subject. "Okay." He took her hand and strode toward the sidewalk that separated the parking lot from the beach. The fast food bag took a quick bank shot into the nearest trash can. He led her off the sidewalk. Shells and stones crunched beneath their feet. At the water's edge, he stopped. The only sound around them came from the soft *whoosh* of the gentle waves. "Tide's coming in," he noted.

"Uh-huh."

God, he hated small talk. His usual approach was to go straight for the jugular. But Summer would only freeze like a winter ice storm if he continued with that delivery. He bent to pick up a smooth, flat stone, then flung it to skip across the sound's surface three times before sinking with a plop.

"How'd you do that?"

He turned to Summer, puzzlement etching his brow. "Skip a rock? You're kidding, right?"

"Nope." She clutched her hands in front of her waist. "In case you haven't noticed, I'm not exactly the athletic type."

"You? The queen of the one-handed Wiffle ball batting stance?" He snorted. "Imagine that."

"I still managed to kick *your* butt that night."

"Puh-leez." He waved a dismissive hand. "I let you win, and you know it."

At last, her perfect lips stretched into an honest-to-goodness happy smile. "Yes, I knew it. So teach me how to skip a rock tonight, and next time I'll let *you* win at Wiffle ball."

"Okay. First, let's find a good stone for skipping." He picked up several, testing their weight and breadth in his palm before selecting two ideal candidates. He handed one to her and kept the second. "Now, hold it with the flat end even between your thumb and fingers."

Her first three attempts failed miserably, sinking before even accomplishing one skip. When the fourth stone didn't even touch water, instead landing about a foot from where they stood, she sighed. "I told you I'm not very athletic."

"You throw like a girl," he replied with a grin.

Fire flashed in her eyes for the briefest moment. "I *am* a girl."

"That explains it then. Here." He stepped behind her, one hand pivoting her at the waist, the other guiding her elbow. "Your stance is wrong." With his chin perched near the crook of her neck, he held his breath to keep from inhaling that familiar roses-and-vanilla scent of her skin. "Now, pull back"—he pulled her arm back and pushed it forward—"and release."

The rock danced over the water's surface—not far, but distance wasn't the objective for this exercise.

"I did it!" She whirled, her face so close he could taste the salt on her lips. Shuddering, she inhaled sharply.

Regret rode heavy on his shoulders as he took a giant step backward. "Yup. You did it. Now let's go celebrate with apple pies."

Chapter Sixteen

"Why do women stay obsessed with men who treat them like garbage?"

At Craig's question, Maureen jerked up her head from the early edition newspapers and frowned. "I thought today's on-air topic was the Hampton Classic. I've been researching all morning—"

"I'm not talking about an on-air conversation," he retorted.

"Oh." She sat back in her chair and looked up at him with an "Aha!" expression. "Trouble at home, Craig? You and the phony missus have a real fight? I warned you about airing that 'kids need boundaries' bit." She curled her fingers around the quote.

"Yeah, you were right. Summer blew a gasket. But that's not what I'm talking about." He swiped the chair from the sports guy's desk and sat across from her. "It's what happened afterward."

"What happened afterward?"

He gave her a brief rundown of finding Summer on the roof, cleaning gutters, and her insistence on repairing the screens.

"Anger mechanism," Maureen remarked through steepled fingers.

"Huh?"

"Some women need an outlet for their anger, particularly if they're not yellers like I am. They'll beat up on inanimate objects instead of the real target of their resentment. Like weeding? That's kinda like pulling someone's hair. Or vacuuming reminds her she keeps going over the same stuff, but no one's listening." He gaped at her, and she grinned. "Dr. Jeff used to talk about anger outlets on that talk show."

"Great. So what does cleaning out gutters on the second story represent?"

"Well, gee, Craig, I don't know. I mean, I'm not an expert. But to me, it would seem like she feels she's in a precarious position."

On a wobbly ladder two stories up, with only Craig to catch her. Made sense. "I can see that. Okay, now here's the part I'm questioning. I took a ride with her yesterday, and we ran into her ex-husband and his new wife. She went whiter than this." He picked up a blank sheet of paper. "I think if I hadn't caught her, she would have swan-dived into the sidewalk. What's that about? I mean, obviously she's still hooked on this bum. And you and I both know he's no good for her."

"We do?"

He ignored her. "And the new wife? There's another piece of work. Snooty little . . ." He paused, seeking the perfect description, and opted for Summer's term from last night. "Snooty little *twit* with her nose in the air because she thinks she won some great big prize. If you ask me, those two deserve each other."

"What did Summer say?"

"Nothing. She was virtually catatonic at that point."

"So you jumped to her defense."

"Someone had to. The new wife had the chains to call Summer pathetic. You believe that?" He picked up a paper clip, began mangling the wire between his fingers. "So I gave them a nice, loud parting shot."

"Nice to hear chivalry's not dead." She took a sip from her coffee mug. "How did Summer react?"

"Like I'd embarrassed her in front of the guy she loves. Which, apparently, I did."

"Which explains your question. But honestly, Craig? I don't know why anyone continues to love the person who's betrayed her. Or him. Every marriage has its own secrets.

You know that. If you really want to know what's up with her and her ex, you should try talking to her."

"I did. I even took her out to dinner afterward, thought I could cheer her up."

"You took her out to dinner." Not a question. In Maureen's infuriating way, she phrased it as a statement, but with an open ending that silently demanded more details.

"She was upset. And anyway, it's not like we went out to some fancy French place. We picked up burgers at a fast food joint."

Maureen's raucous laughter echoed through the office like a flock of rabid parrots. "Oh my God, you're in love!"

He fumbled the paper clip, hurriedly looked around the office. Thank God no one was around to overhear her. "You've gone insane," he said through his teeth.

"Oh, please." She brushed a hand at him. "I've known you . . . what? Twelve years now?"

"And your expertise about me says a quickie burger and fries means I'm in love? You're way off, Maureen. *Way* off."

"Really?" She leaned forward, eyes narrowed. "When was the last time you had a quickie burger and fries without your kids?"

"Leave my kids out of this."

Smiling, she leaned back again and folded her arms over her chest. "I rest my case."

"What case? My family's off-limits in this discussion, and you know it."

"Yep, your family's off-limits to everyone. And yet, you let Summer in."

"Of course I let her in. She's taking care of my family, the house, even my gutters."

"No, you idiot. You let her in to the real you. In the twelve years I've known you, I've been to your house twice." She held up two fingers. "Lenny's *never* been there. You protect your private life better than the CIA guards spy secrets. And that's fine. We all respect that. So if you come in and tell me your housekeeper's upset over her ex-husband's new bride, and you took her to some fancy French place to make her feel better, I don't think twice about it. 'Cuz that's not who you are or what you do deep down. But burgers and fries? Walks on the beach with the dog? School plays and Little League games? That's the real you. So either you're extremely interested in this woman, or the devil's shopping for snow-shoes right now."

He pushed off her desk, got to his shaky legs. "You're off the deep end." Noting the ON AIR light go off, he headed for the studio. "And this stays off the airwaves, by the way."

"Of course it does," she replied with a cackle.

In love. He shoved his way into the studio. God help him.

No matter how many trips Lyn took to New York City and Long Island, she never got used to the gridlock. In her sleepy Vermont town, a traffic jam occurred only when Arthur Kinsey drove his tractor half a mile on Route 2 to travel from one side of his dairy farm to the other. In winter, locals knew to avoid the roads leading to the ski resorts at peak time—from eight to ten in the morning and four to six in the afternoon. June through September, residents detoured around the highways where boat ramps and white-water-rafting businesses flourished. Autumn brought the leaf peepers, who, without warning, were known to hit the brakes to gawk at a particularly colorful tree or vista. Never, however, did traffic come to a complete standstill in her neighborhood.

But down here, hours and seasons seemed to hold no sway over the crowds and snarls of cars idling on the highways. Last time she'd made this trip, Lyn had driven down in the middle of the night, thinking to outwit the traffic demons. No dice. The Long Island Expressway was closed from ten P.M. to six A.M. Construction crews worked on fifteen miles of the Island's main artery, which required drivers to settle for the stop-and-go crawl on the service road for a dozen exits. Stuck among them, Lyn suffered a delay of nearly an hour before she reached April's house. And dagnabbit, she didn't want another hour in the car today. After five hours with nothing but Top 20 music on the radio to distract her thoughts, she really needed to talk to someone.

Unfortunately, unless she wanted to roll down her window and shout at the driver stalled next to her, she had no choice but to sit and stew. Ideas tumbled through her head in freefall. All of them focused on Doug Sawyer, the man who gave her a thousand reasons to smile every day. Much as she loved him, she hated the distance that always existed between them. Because, when not in pursuit of another sports story, he normally lived in Manhattan. She, on the other hand, owned a bed-and-breakfast in Vermont. The time had come to put an end to this long-distance relationship once and for all.

Yet again, the brake lights blared from the vehicle in front of her, and she pressed her foot down to stop her car's snail-paced forward motion. For heaven's sake, she could see her exit from here. So near, yet so far. She squirmed, peeling her skin off the seat where too many hours in the same position caused her bare thighs to stick to the leather.

On her left, a motorcyclist zipped between the lanes of standstill cars. Idiot. He probably wanted to beat the bad weather. Dark storm clouds had gathered overhead, heralding the imminent arrival of one of those violent afternoon summer thunderstorms prevalent when Long Island humidity reached saturation point.

Still, didn't the biker realize how easily he could lose a limb with such a stupid maneuver? In the last year, Ski-Hab, the rehabilitation program for amputees she'd helped establish at home, had worked with six motorcycle accident victims. Ask them now if that shortcut or quick jump at the light was worth losing a limb or two.

Traffic inched up again, and slowly Lyn eased onto the opening for her exit ramp. Fifteen minutes later, she pulled into her sister's driveway. As she stepped out of the car, her nephew burst from the front door.

"Aunt Lyn, can I take your luggage?"

Wow. He'd grown taller since the last time she'd visited and now stood at her height, but stockier in build. Pretty soon he'd tower over her. Michael's eager doe eyes, so adorable when he was a toddler, these days clearly showed he was a young man with Down syndrome.

"Can I have a hug first?" she asked. "Or are you too old to show public affection to your aunt?"

In response, the teen flung his arms around her with so much exuberance, he knocked her off-balance and stole her breath.

"Whoa, easy, Mike." God, the kid had the strength and bulk of a bear. "You're gonna crack my ribs."

"Sorry." He eased up enough to allow her a shallow inhale.

"That's okay." Stepping away from his boa constrictor embrace, she ruffled his sandy hair. "I'm thrilled you're excited to see me. So what's new in your life? Got a girlfriend yet?"

"No, but I got a job." A spot of spittle glistened on his grinning lips, and Lyn averted her gaze to ward off a shudder.

When she looked up at the white, raised ranch-style house, she spotted Jeff at the front door, watching their exchange.

Lyn nodded a hello, then turned back to Michael. "You got a job?" April was probably beside herself, partly proud of her son's growing independence, but terrified, knowing he'd never be fully able to live on his own. "That's terrific. Where?"

"At Home Stop. You know, the store where Mom buys all her sheets and towels? Especially the fancy ones for company like you?"

"I rate fancy towels?" she remarked. "Yowza. That's two compliments for me already, and I haven't even left the driveway yet."

The wind kicked up damp air and whistled through her ears.

"Rain's coming," Jeff called to them. "You two planning to come inside, or do we have to build a shelter around you?"

Lyn laughed. "Come on. Walk me inside, and you can tell me about the job."

"First," Mike said as he raced to the trunk, "your luggage. It's good practice for me. Except I usually put stuff *in* a car, not pull stuff out."

As he chattered about his new job, where he helped carry heavy items for customers and corralled shopping carts, she popped her trunk and allowed him to retrieve her suitcase.

By the time they reached the front porch overhang, the first fat raindrops hit the slate stones at her feet.

"Hurry." Jeff swung open the storm door and ushered them inside. Once they stepped into the foyer, he quickly sealed the house from the suddenly torrential rain. "Michael, take Aunt Lyn's suitcase into the spare room, then go get ready for work. I'll drive you."

"Okay."

While Michael lumbered upstairs with her suitcase, Jeff turned to her. "Lyn, what can I get you?"

"Iced tea would be great."

He shot his fingers at her. "You got it. Have a seat in the den while I grab a couple of glasses."

Purse slung on one shoulder, she stepped into the cozy den, where Jeff had already turned on the brass wall sconces over the unlit brick fireplace. Outside, the afternoon had turned dark as night. As she settled onto the plush sectional farthest from the window, she glanced up at the mantel. Jeff and April's engagement photo smiled down on her. April's smile glowed almost nuclear, and her eyes glistened. Jeff, arm wrapped possessively around her, beamed with pride. Lyn had never seen her sister look so blissfully happy, so . . . *loved*.

"Where's April?" she called to Jeff.

He popped up beside her, holding two glasses filled with iced tea. After offering her one, he took a seat in the club chair opposite with the second. "She got hung up at the office. Emergency with one of the clients."

"Oh, God," Lyn blurted. "Not Summer?" Not that she'd

blame Summer if something happened between her and that awful Cliff Hanger.

Jeff laughed. "No. But that was my first reaction too. This crisis had something to do with two sweet-sixteen parties booked on the same night with the same catering staff. April will have it all sorted out in no time."

Thunder cracked loud enough to rattle the picture window, and Lyn flinched. To cover her fear, she asked about April's daughter, away at college, but expected to arrive to be maid of honor for the wedding. "Becky's not home yet?"

Leaning back in his chair, he sipped from his glass. "She had one more class she couldn't miss, so she's driving home tonight."

"Tell her to avoid the L.I.E. after ten. That construction zone will kill her."

"She knows. She got caught in it last month." He cocked his head, solemn gray eyes studious and penetrating. "Is something wrong, Lyn? Besides the traffic? Is it the press? I've already chased two reporters off the lawn today. And it's only going to get worse between now and Sunday."

Bless him. He really did understand how the paparazzi used to terrorize her. "No. I know that."

"Do you want me to call April and get you another house-sitting gig?"

His banal tone held no judgment, yet the heat of shame crept into her cheeks just the same, and she sipped her iced tea to cool the burn. Eighteen months ago, after years of solitude, the press had tracked her now-famous sister and Jeff to her inn. Lyn had escaped the throng of reporters, including Doug, thanks to April's assistant, Brenda. A generous client of Rainey-Day-Wife had allowed her to use his home for a hideaway in exchange for house- and pet-sitting services.

"No."

That time in her life—the panic, the utter hatred for reporters—was behind her. Thanks, almost entirely, to Doug. Which brought her full circle to the issue that had distracted her all the way here.

"Can I tell you a secret?"

He shrugged, took another sip, swallowed. "Secrets are my business."

"You can't tell April."

"Okay." He held out his hand, palm up. "But give me a dollar first."

On instinct, she clutched her purse tighter. "What?"

"Just like a lawyer. You give me a dollar, and you're not my sister-in-law. You're a patient. I can't divulge anything you tell me."

Cute. And sweet that he thought to protect her. "Well, it's not *that* dire. Everyone will know soon enough. I just want to run it past someone else before I make a total fool of myself."

His eyes narrowed, and he slid to the edge of the chair, leaning his elbows on his knees. "This isn't going to get me in trouble, is it? You're not planning something illegal, are you?"

She stifled a giggle. "No, silly. I want to ask Doug to marry me."

"Oh, well, that's different." His posture relaxed, and a wide grin spread across his face. "Since you're fairly glowing when you mention the word marriage, I'm assuming you're not asking me to help you sort out your feelings first."

"Definitely not. At least, not about the marriage part. Doug and I have been sort of dancing around the subject for months now. The thing is, I don't know how or when to pop the question. These days, we're rarely in the same state." She furrowed her brow, and her lips quirked. "Except for this weekend."

He spread his hands wide. "So do it this weekend."

"No." She shook her head hard enough to dislocate her brain. "No way."

"Why not?"

Was he crazy? "Because this weekend is all about you and April."

His sudden burst of laughter only deepened her concern for his sanity. "The last thing we want is for this weekend to be about just us. This weekend is about *love,* Lyn. Love and second chances. Don't you think that makes it a perfect time for you to take your own second chance?"

Her lips tightened as she played with the idea in her head. Just because Jeff could talk the devil into random acts of kindness didn't mean she took him at his word. After all, April might feel differently about Lyn and Doug stealing a little of her spotlight. She glanced at the photo on the mantel. At the beautiful, generous, happy woman who smiled out at her.

Okay, it was a long shot. Still . . .

Her mother would have a fit. If Lyn proposed to Doug at April's wedding on Sunday, Mom would automatically accuse her of jealousy. At the very least, bad manners, which in Susan Raine's world was almost as serious as murder.

But there was another option. Mom had already backed out of Saturday night's revelries because of the late hour. She never ate dinner after five P.M., citing a delicate stomach. Yeah, right. Like anything about Iron Mom could be considered delicate.

"Maybe," Lyn said aloud, "at the rehearsal dinner."

Chapter Seventeen

Summer glanced out the window at the teeming rain, and then frowned at Craig, who stood near the front door, shrugging into a tan windbreaker. "I thought practice would be canceled. Have you looked outside lately?"

Although the clock on the cable box in the den plainly glowed 4:08 in neon green, outside, the day had blackened to resemble midnight. The rain hit the ground with so much force, mud splashed upward, spattering the sidewalk and tree trunks.

"Why?" Craig pushed the curtain aside and peered into the gloom, then turned back to Summer. "Have you seen any lightning?"

Lightning? They had to wait for lightning before insisting Nate stay home? "Well, no, but—"

"Any of the coaches call to tell us practice is off?" he persisted.

"No."

He slapped his hands at his sides. "Then Nate has football practice."

"Even if it's pouring rain?" Folding her arms over her chest, she shot her weight to one hip. This whole argument was ridiculous. What parent in his right mind would allow his child outdoors in this tempest?

"Have you ever watched a football game? Those guys play in rain, snow, and twenty-below temperatures."

Oh, for heaven's sake. "They also get paid millions to do so." She jabbed her index finger toward Nate, who stood on

133

jumpy legs, watching the adults argue. "But this is a little boy, not an overpaid bear of a man."

Beside her, Nate clucked his tongue and rolled his eyes.

She leaned toward the pouting boy. "Sorry, but it's true."

Craig yanked up the windbreaker's zipper with a fist. "Do you think I'd allow any harm to come to *my* son?"

His open hostility dragged her attention away from Nate's indignation and back to her own. "Not intentionally."

On a deep exhale, he shook his head. "Listen, Summer. I'm really sorry. I know you didn't sign up for this, but my attorney can only squeeze me in this afternoon."

She waved him off. Did he really think she only argued about dragging a child out to play in the rain because she'd be inconvenienced? "That's the nature of the beast. I knew my hours wouldn't be nine to five when I signed up with Rainey-Day-Wife."

So did April, who didn't voice a single complaint about postponing this afternoon's appointment with the florist. Dinner afterward, however, was still scheduled for seven thirty with the rest of the girls in the bridal party: April's daughter, Becky; Lyn; and Jeff's sister, Lauren.

"Summer, you've been a godsend to me. Honestly. So if you want to bail, I'll understand." He picked up an accordion file from the cocktail table.

Meanwhile, Summer watched the rain pelt the window. "No. I've got this under control." Maybe they should skip football practice and start building an ark.

"My meeting shouldn't last more than an hour," he said at last. "Then I'll race over to the football field to relieve you. Hopefully, I'll get there before the scrimmage." He cocked his head, eyes narrowed. "Are you sure you're okay with this?"

Summer looked down at Nate's distressed expression and forced a confident smile, far from the doubts swimming in her head. "Of course."

Nate's joy filled the room as he clapped and hissed out, "Yessssss!"

Craig grinned, relief evident in his relaxed brow. "Great.

Dad will help you get Nate's gear together. And there's a golf umbrella in the garage, a big white thing with the radio station's call letters in royal blue. It's ridiculous-looking, but it'll keep you dry so long as the wind doesn't pick up and slant the rain sideways."

From the comfort of the den, Summer stared at the oak tree at the end of the driveway. Branches whipped and snapped. Terrific. Even if Craig got to the field thirty minutes after practice began, she'd be a soggy mess. Unless she wrapped herself in a plastic tarp.

He must have read the misgivings on her face because he added, "You could stay in the car if you want. Just let one of the coaches know where you are—"

"No." She might not know a lot about football, but she'd seen enough of the games Brad used to watch to understand the high injury rate. No way would she sit warm and dry in a car while this man's little boy—a child she was responsible for—risked coming down with the flu, or worse, a broken bone. *Another* broken bone. She shot a glance toward Scott, who sat on the couch, crutches leaning against the end table. One fracture in the household was enough right now.

"Okay then." Craig turned toward the door. "I'll get to the field as soon as I can. And Summer?" His tone softened to silk. "Thank you. You've saved my life. Again. It's becoming a regular occurrence."

His gratitude melted her steel exterior. A frisson of warmth heated her bare arms. "You're welcome."

When he left the house, she turned to Nate. "Get your gear, kiddo. I'm taking you to football practice."

With a whoop of delight, the boy raced down the hallway toward his bedroom.

Well, at least one of them was happy at this turn of events.

Craig sat in the attorney's waiting room and forced his gaze to focus on the article in the news magazine. No luck. Regardless of how hard he stared, all he saw were foreign characters, like ants that scurried all over the page. Dread had stolen his intellect. Only one sentence echoed in the abyss inside his head. The voice of Clark Lantz, Attorney-at-Law, on the phone this morning. *Your ex-wife's intending to go forward with her request for full custody.*

Full custody.

And as the mother, she'd probably win. The only reason she hadn't received custody at the time of the divorce was because she hadn't asked. Chelsea wasn't a bad mother. Craig had never doubted her devotion to Nate, Scott, and Maddie. As a wife? Well, her loyalty remained firmly with herself. The minute she realized Craig had no intention of capitalizing on his notoriety like some other syndicated radio hosts, she'd begun looking for better alternatives.

Under his breath he cursed her and himself for dragging three innocent victims through their melodrama. Lantz's secretary, a woman of a certain age and formidable attitude, stared at him over the spectacles perched on the edge of her eagle-beak nose. Had she heard him?

Craig fought the urge to squirm like a schoolboy being stared down by the principal. In all her years here she must have heard worse from some of Lantz's clients. Lawyers didn't exactly give people the warm fuzzies.

The door to the attorney's office opened. "Craig?" Clark Lantz stood on the threshold in his blue pin-striped Armani suit, white shirt, and red silk power tie. "Come on in."

He looked in control, confident, and crisp. Meanwhile, Craig more closely resembled a sodden dishrag, shabby and wrung out. How many of his billable hours of misery had paid for this guy's wardrobe?

On shaky legs, Craig rose, hands clutching the file folder that contained all his divorce papers like a drowning man with a life preserver. Once again, he cursed Chelsea for putting them all through this. This time, however, he made sure not to utter the thought aloud. With a nod as he passed the attorney, he stumbled into the office. He settled in the chair in front of the sleek, polished desk, facing the tremendous wall of law books.

As the door closed with a click, Lantz's shadow fell over the gleaming desktop. "How've you been, Craig?"

Craig held up a hand. "Don't."

The attorney sat across from him, his brow wrinkled in puzzlement.

"Don't play the small-talk card. Just give it to me straight. What's it going to take for me to keep my kids?" He searched the desktop for a paper clip, a pushpin, a speck of dust—anything to keep from twitching.

"Slow down, Craig." Lantz slowly bounced his hands as if attempting to calm a lunatic. "She hasn't filed a motion yet. She simply told her attorney she's considering the idea. I wouldn't have even known except Stuart mentioned it on the sixteenth hole two days ago."

"How lucky for me." Of course his attorney and his ex-wife's attorney played golf together. Another of God's cruel jokes at his expense.

"It *is* lucky for you." Lantz leaned back and laced his hands behind his head. "This is your chance for a preemptive strike."

Craig's lips twisted in disbelief. "How?"

"You know her better than anyone. She's your ex-wife. So talk to her. Find out what put this idea in her head after all these years. Then figure out a way to dislodge it."

"I already know what put this idea in her head. She thinks I'm incompetent as a parent." Before Lantz could say anything, he added, "And I've already taken steps to fix it."

Lantz sat up and folded his hands on the desktop. "You have? Well, good for you. But does Chelsea know that?"

"Of course not. I only hired Summer a month ago. We're still breaking each other in."

"Breaking each other . . . ?" He shook his head and waved away whatever he'd been about to say. "Forget it. I don't want to know."

"Oh, grow up," Craig snapped. "She's a nanny."

"Is that all she is?"

Craig's hands fisted tightly around the folder. In the silence of this legal sanctum, the papers inside crinkled louder than machine-gun fire. Calling Summer a lifesaver was probably closer to the truth. "Well, no. She does a lot more for my dad and me."

"For . . . ?" He visibly swallowed. "Your *dad* and you?"

"Yeah, she's taken over the housekeeping, the meals, the kids' practices. She got my daughter enrolled in preschool. She even fixed my gutters. She's been a godsend for us." He paused, cocked his head to study the lawyer the way an owl would give a wounded mouse the once-over. *Pompous idiot. Say anything you want about me, but leave Summer out of it. She's the best thing that's ever happened to me—to us. Even when I've thrown her a curve, like today. Go ahead. Insult her. I dare you.* "What'd you think I meant?"

"Nothing." Lantz's expression blanked. "Look, Craig, I'm trying to do you a favor here. I know you really don't want to go to court over this. Aside from the expense, I can tell you from past experience these things get ugly fast. So finish breaking in your nanny—or whatever she is and whatever you're doing to her—then get in touch with Chelsea. Assure her things are perfect the way they are, and see if you can calm her down before she has Stuart file any paperwork."

Assure her things were perfect? He thought of Summer in the rain at the football field and . . .

Oh, shinola. He'd forgotten to tell her to bring a chair.

Perfect.

Yeah, right.

Chapter Eighteen

Summer huddled underneath the umbrella and longed for a hot bath, a glass of wine, and a roof over her head. As the rain sloshed her ankles, she reconsidered. Walls would be nice, too. And maybe a place to sit. In his haste to make the meeting with his attorney, Craig had neglected to mention she'd need a chair, since the field the teams used had no bleachers or benches of any kind.

Not that she'd consider this war zone a field. Parents huddled behind a battered, low chain-link fence on a torn-up scrap of weeds that ran the length of the football field but was only about six feet across at its widest. No buildings buffered the wind except a black rental storage container that housed the football equipment when not in use. There was no concession stand, not even bathrooms. Twice now, she'd seen kids leave the practice area to duck into the woods beyond them, then return a few minutes later, tucking their jerseys into their pants. Summer didn't need to be that Madden guy to figure out what the kids were doing back there.

She shivered, from a combination of disgust and the effects of standing too long in the rain. The air was so heavy and wet that after the first twenty minutes here, her lungs struggled to breathe without sucking in the moisture. She didn't know how Nate could run around in his heavy football gear, made even heavier thanks to the deluge of rainwater, without passing out. In the last ninety minutes, the children had only taken two breaks. Both times, Nate had collapsed on the muddy grass near his minicooler, popped out his mouth guard, removed his helmet to reveal wet hair plastered to his head, and gasped for breath before chugging water from a sports bottle.

And on her game tally, score another point for the wrong shoes. With every step, her heels sank into thick mud, and then required herculean effort to pull them back out. Her best summer sandals, pale pink suede with short spiky heels that did wonders for her legs, were now ruined beyond redemption. In hindsight, she should have opted for boots, or those hip waders fishermen wore.

As she shifted her weight from one foot to the other, she studied the hundreds of little boys—and a few girls!—scrabbling around the muddy field. Broken into groups by age and then again by physical ability, the children began practice by running laps. After they'd huffed and puffed their way around the gridiron's entire perimeter, one group hit their shoulders into a bizarre steel structure that resembled a farmer's thresher. Several lines of children crashed into each other, shoulder pads crunching, again and again. Yet another cluster of players crawled like crabs on the ground.

She couldn't tell which team Nate belonged to. They all looked the same: black helmets emblazoned with large silver stars, black mesh practice jerseys, shiny tight white pants. Who on earth decided football pants should be white? A marketing executive for the bleach industry? Because as she looked at all the mud and grass stains across the knees and backsides of the children, she despaired that those pants would never know white again.

Only their shoes varied—no, not shoes. Nate had called them cleats. Some kids wore black cleats with white trim, some had more white and less black, and one kid even had traffic-cone-orange cleats. No doubt his parents knew where he was every second on the field. Lucky them.

Everywhere around these clusters of children, coaches urged them on with quick blasts of whistles and orders of "Harder," "Faster," "Get up and do it again." Dozens of loud, overweight dads seemed to relive their own dashed fantasies through these poor soggy youngsters. Did their wives dare to argue against their children participating in such a violent sport? In the circle nearest where she stood, two players crashed into each other with a heart-wrenching crack. Summer winced. Why on earth would a mother willingly sign up her child for potential injury? Some of the boys and girls were so young, nearly babies.

On a sigh, she glanced at her watch. 6:45. If Craig showed up at this very minute, she'd have just enough time to run back to the house and change her clothes before meeting the girls at Riff's Grill. Her hair, no doubt a sodden disaster by now, would have to air dry during the car ride.

"Well, hello there," a deep voice said from behind her.

She turned to find a stocky bulldog of a man in hooded, clear plastic raingear smiling at her. His eyes held a wolf's gleam. A groan rose to her lips, and she tightened her jaw to keep the noise in check. Really? A pick-up artist on the pee-wee football field? Dressed in her mother's couch covering?

"I don't remember seeing *you* at the parents meeting. I'm Paul. Paul Hobart. My son, Mark, is on the nine-year-old A team. You?"

She looked down at him, not difficult since she topped him by a good six inches. The nine-year-old A team. Nate's team. Fabulous. She sighed her defeat. Okay. For Nate's sake—and his father's—she'd be pleasant to this man. But if he didn't stop staring at her chest, she was going to deck him.

"I'm Summer," she said blandly.

"A lovely name for a lovely woman."

Ick. The groan would have escaped if Summer hadn't tightened every muscle in her face. "Thank you."

"Whose mom are you, Summer?"

No one's. She almost clasped her belly as she always did when she remembered the hysterectomy. Instead, she gripped the umbrella handle with both hands. She'd never be anyone's mom. Case closed. "I'm here with Nate Hartmann."

"You're Nate's mom?"

"No, I'm his . . ." She paused. What *was* she exactly? Not

a babysitter. Not a maid. Not really a caregiver. Technically, she was all of those and yet none of those. "I'm helping out the family until Craig's father is back on his feet."

"So, what? Like a nanny?"

"No. Like a very good friend." At the sound of Craig's intrusion into the conversation, Summer relaxed. Finally, her white knight had arrived.

"Hey, Craig." Paul greeted him with a quick head jerk.

"Paul." Craig stepped closer to Summer and ducked his head under the umbrella. "Got room in here for me, sweetheart?"

Sweetheart? A few days ago, she was "just an employee." Now she was his "sweetheart"? But since his new term for her suited her desire to fend off Mr. Hobart, she'd play along.

"For you?" She beamed and pulled him closer to shield them both from the storm's deluge. "Of course."

"Sorry I'm late," he told her.

"That's o—" Before she finished the statement, his mouth crushed her lips.

His kiss was soft, tender, and *wow*. Delicious. Inside Summer, the woman who'd gone without affection for such a long time roused from her postdivorce coma. She lost herself in the whirl of sensations: the warmth that rose in her cheeks and throat, her suddenly pounding heart, the comfort of his arm around her waist.

Too soon, he released her and winked. "How's Nate doing?"

Nate? Oh, right. A dense fog muddled her senses. "Umm . . . fine." She couldn't seem to calm her racing heart or find her balance.

Meanwhile, all the confidence fled from Paul's tone as he kicked at a clod of weeds at his feet. "Okay, then. Nice talking to you, Summer."

Craig hauled her close until her butt fit nicely into the curve of his hip and abdomen. Every nerve ending in her body jumped and twitched, short-circuiting her brain. She practically melted into his arms.

"Say something, sweetheart," he murmured, his breath hot against her nape.

Her knees shook, and if he hadn't held her so tightly, she might have sunk into the mud. Somehow, she managed to find her voice, shaky as it was. "N-nice to m-meet you, Paul."

"See you around, Paul," Craig said, while his face nuzzled her neck.

"Yeah," Paul muttered. "Right." He turned and strode away.

Once they were alone, Craig took a step back. For a moment, Summer stood like a mannequin, unable to move or breathe. At last, awareness returned in small ticks of time. *Holy moly, what just happened?* She blinked, trying to regain focus.

Craig still stood under the umbrella, but barely. "Sorry about the frontal assault, Summer. The thing is, that guy? Hobart? He's a lech."

She inhaled, welcoming the heavy moisture as deep and cleansing. Thank God his sudden show of affection was just a ruse. She could deal with a ruse better than with the alternative.

"Don't apologize," she blurted. "You handled that well."

"I did?" He sounded surprised. "Hmm . . . maybe I should accost pretty ladies more often. Double bonus if I managed to get Paul outta here and gain your appreciation at the same time. I feel kinda like Superman."

She widened her eyes and furiously batted her lashes. "My hero."

"You're welcome." With his hand curled, he blew on his fingers, then pretended to buff them on his shirtfront.

"How was the meeting with the lawyer?"

He stiffened instantly, and his expression darkened. "Later. Not here."

Of course. How stupid of her. He wouldn't discuss anything so personal in such a public place. Neither would she. "I'm sorry."

He didn't react to her apology. Instead, he jerked his head

toward the parking lot. "You should go. I hope I didn't make you too late."

Too late? Oh, shoot. April's bridal party dinner.

Craig watched Summer sprint toward her car, rain pelting her like buckshot on a deer. She'd insisted he keep the umbrella, not just for himself, but for Nate. His gaze strayed to the field, and he shook his head. Ridiculous. Nate was already covered head to toe in mud. In fact, he might have to hit the boy with the garden hose before letting him inside the house. Forget his minivan. The upholstery was doomed.

Summer had insisted, though. So he'd given in.

He'd give her just about anything right now. Anything that would convince her to stay with them until Chelsea's threat couldn't come to fruition.

Thank God he hadn't blown the whole setup when he kissed her. Lucky for him she'd understood his subterfuge, if not the full reason behind it.

Yes, Paul Hobart was a lech. But Paul Hobart was a lech with a particular fondness for nannies. He and his wife had divorced when he'd been caught having an affair with the babysitter from next door. Six months later, he dumped the neighbor for his ex-wife's new au pair, a young student from Russia who barely spoke English but openly worshipped Paul.

No way would Craig allow Hobart within ten feet of Summer. Not that he had any say over who Summer dated. She could date anyone she wanted. *After* Chelsea saw reason. And not Paul Hobart. Ever. She was too good for that weasel.

Too good for me too, he thought ruefully.

Which really sucked wind, because he had definitely enjoyed that kiss. One more glance in her direction as she climbed into her Escalade. He sighed, then turned his attention to his son sliding across the field face-first on his chest. A muddy wall of water rose up around the boy like a tsunami. The kid's uniform pants would be permanently tan by the time they left the field tonight. He cast one last look at the parking lot. The Escalade's taillights lit up the dark as Summer drove away.

My hero. She'd been teasing, but if an opening popped up to fill that position, he'd leap at the opportunity to be her true hero. When he thought about how she'd wound up in his life, under his roof, he'd consider her more like his miracle. Her arrival had made his life easier, less stressful and more fun. Forget employee. Summer was, as he'd told Paul, a very good friend.

A friend he desperately needed to stick around for a while, at least until Chelsea came to her senses.

You're in big trouble, pal. It's not like you're married to her. Face it, someone as perfect as Summer would never be interested in a nine-to-five schlub with three kids and a live-in dad for baggage. You'd better come up with a reason to make her stay. Fast.

What was keeping Summer?

April cast another worried glance at the entrance to Riff's Grill. A stickler for punctuality, Summer was never late.

"Hell-o?" Becky, seated beside her, waved a hand in April's face. "Mom, are you listening to me?"

"Huh?" She refocused on her daughter and the other ladies at the table: her sister Lyn and Jeff's sister, Lauren. A college student, an innkeeper, and a captain of industry. No doubt about it, she'd amassed a very diverse group of women for her bridal party.

"I asked if we have room at the house for Ace to stay until after the wedding," Becky said with enough sharpness in her voice to cut diamonds.

April frowned as she considered the logistics. Lyn already had the spare bedroom. And honestly? She really didn't want Ace Riordan, professional snowboarding's Aerial Snowball, under the same roof as her smitten daughter for three days. "I think he's fine at Doug's place," she replied.

Lyn's sweetie had a two-bedroom on the Upper East

Side. And since Ace and Doug were already friends, neither felt put out by the idea.

Becky, on the other hand, couldn't hide her disappointment. "All the way in Manhattan? We don't get to spend enough time together."

Exactly.

A flurry near the restaurant's entrance cut off her reply. About time Summer showed up. Sure enough, the maître d' pointed at their table. April rose to wave her over. But as Summer stepped into the bright lights of the dining room, April's jaw fell. "Summer?"

In thirty years April had never seen her sister appear in public without the perfect hair, the perfect outfit, the perfect accessories. Until now. Wet cats looked sleeker. Her normally fluffed and gorgeous hair stuck out in damp, spiky curls. Mascara ringed the area under her eyes and spotted her upper cheekbones. Her pink-and-white-striped ruffled blouse lay against her body like a wet towel, limp and lifeless. Brown spots flecked her pale pink skirt.

Mud? On Summer? Even as a child, Summer never got dirty.

"Oh my God, are you okay? Did the car break down?" She gasped. "Were you in an accident?"

"Don't fuss, April," Summer scolded. With a huff, she dropped into the nearest empty chair. "No accident, no breakdown. I just ran late at football practice with Nate and didn't have time to go home and change."

Lyn sat up and leaned into view. "*You* were at a football game? In this weather?"

Summer's expression turned sour. "First of all, it was practice. And secondly, as I became acutely aware this evening, unless there's lightning, the show must go on."

"You poor thing," Lauren exclaimed as she rose. "Here, take my seat. It's farthest from the air-conditioning vents."

April shot her future sister-in-law a grateful look. Before their first meeting, she'd been prepared for an entirely different woman. Based on Jeff's comments about his only sister, heir to the family's vast corporate entity, she'd envisioned someone brash, masculine, and pushy. Lauren, to her surprise, was none of those things. At least, not with her. She *did* show a competitive streak with Jeff, who always took the barbs in stride. The consummate psychologist wouldn't rise to sibling rivalry.

She studied her sisters with jaundiced eyes. The Raine girls had always thrived on jealousy and vying for favored-nation status with their parents. Only in the last two years had they put aside their pettiness. In dealing with their own issues, each woman had learned to appreciate her sisters for their strengths rather than harping on their differences.

While Lauren and Summer switched seats, the waiter approached. "Miss, can I get you something to drink?"

"Hot t-tea," Summer told him through chattering teeth. "W-with lemon. Thanks."

"Here, Aunt Summer." Becky shrugged off her hooded college sweatshirt. "Take this."

A wave of guilt washed over April. Summer had called earlier to cancel their appointment with the florist, and she'd praised Summer for putting the Hartmanns' priorities before her own. Was she responsible for the way Summer looked right now—wet, chilled, and miserable? Had she somehow guilted Summer into spending time out in the rain for a man who didn't have the sense to properly care for his kids?

Before her conscience could swamp her, she turned to her sister. "I'm sorry, Sum."

Huddled in Becky's bulky gray hoodie, Summer looked up, eyes wide. "What on earth for?"

"I shouldn't have pushed to involve you with Craig Hartmann. At the time, I thought since you needed a place to live and he needed a live-in caretaker, you were perfect for each other."

Summer offered a weak smile and picked up an artfully folded napkin from the place setting beside her. "We are. Craig's a good man, his kids are sweet, I like his dad, and they all need me."

April shook her head. "I didn't expect you to become a slave to the household, Sum."

"I'm not." Once she draped the napkin on her lap, she leaned forward, hands clasped on the tablecloth. "For the first time in aeons, I feel *needed*. Do you have any idea how much that means to me?"

"Not at the expense of your health and well-being," April retorted. "First thing tomorrow, I'm going to officially pull you from that job and—"

Summer's palms hit the table with so much force, the silverware clattered. "Don't you dare assign someone else to *my* family. You got that? This has nothing to do with you. Stop trying to control everyone and everything, April."

"Yeah," Lyn chimed in. "That's Summer's job. And she's darn good at it, by golly."

"Look who's talking," Summer rejoined with a grin. "The girl afraid of her own shadow."

"Not anymore," Lyn replied. "Falling in love with a reporter got me over my fear of the press in a big way."

"And falling in love with a psychologist gave her a new outlook on life," Summer added with a head jerk in April's direction. "Lucky for me, I'm perfect the way I am, thank you very much. I don't need a man to help me see the problems in my life."

"Oh, really?" Lyn arched a brow. "I wouldn't sound so smug if I were you. I'd be willing to bet something else besides being needed makes you want to stay with your family, snookums."

Summer's gaze dropped to her lap, and her fingers fussed with the napkin. "Like what?"

"Like a fluttery feeling in your stomach when he's in the same room?" Lyn suggested.

Of course. Leave it to Lyn to pick up on a possible attraction between Summer and Craig Hartmann. As the idea took root in her fertile brain, April couldn't resist adding fertilizer to this seedling. "Is that why you have a goofy smile on your face whenever Craig Hartmann's name comes up?"

Summer's head shot up like a rocket at blastoff. "I do not!"

"Wow," Lauren interjected. "That was a pretty quick denial. Tells me they're either on to something or you really hate the guy. Which is it?"

"Craig and I have an ideal employee/employer relationship. Nothing more," Summer replied.

The waiter reappeared, and she grabbed the china teacup before he could place it on the table.

"Oh, I don't know about that," Lyn said with a grin. "The lady doth protest too much, methinks."

"Tell us, Summer. Do the stupidest things remind you of him?" Lauren pressed. "You know, rain on a window, puppies playing in the grass, a cool breeze on a hot day . . . ?" Her eyes took on a dreamy quality.

Well, I'll be darned. April suddenly realized that, despite Jeff's beliefs to the contrary, Lauren was romantically involved with a person, and not just the family business.

Once again, April's gaze circled the table. Lyn loved Doug. Summer might be falling for Craig Hartmann. Lauren definitely had someone in her radar. And Becky had a thing for Ace. Apparently, in this henhouse, love was in the air. Wonderful, wonderful love.

Summer sipped her tea before replying, "You're all being ridiculous."

Maybe, April thought as she studied the bloom rising in her sister's cheeks. *Then again, maybe not.*

She'd bet her business that the fresh color on Summer's face had nothing to do with hot tea.

Chapter Nineteen

Summer's to-do list for the next day was a godsend. With so many details to see to before April's wedding tomorrow, she had no time to review the nonsense from the ladies last night. All those stupid veiled hints about her and Craig. Like a man and a woman couldn't have a friendship without there being some kind of physical attraction between them. How absurd. Sure, she liked Craig. And yes, he was extremely attractive—inside and out. If she wanted a relationship, he'd definitely be the man she pursued. But really, with so much on her plate, she wouldn't add a heaping spoonful of romance right now.

In the future . . . ? Who could tell? Once she had her business off the ground and no longer worked for Rainey-Day-Wife, or *Craig* for that matter, she might find a way to bump into him again. Until then, she'd focus on the party at hand.

After brewing a cup of coffee for fortitude for the day ahead, she picked up her trusty lined pad from the kitchen counter and studied the first few chores listed on page one.

Confirmations: bakery, hair and makeup, limos, florist, minister.
Pickups: favors (to be dropped off at the hall before 2 pm today!)
Create: payment envelopes, emergency kit . . .

A rap on her door drew her gaze up.
"Summer? Can I come in?"

Craig.

She opened the door to find him lounging against the door-jamb. He looked totally relaxed—no more dark rings under those fabulous eyes—and adorable in his usual faded-T-shirt-and-jeans ensemble. His feet were bare, adding a boyish quality that melted her businesslike composure to mush.

"Hi." *God, that was a dumb thing to say.* Resisting the urge to smooth her hair, she tightened her hold on her notepad. She ushered him inside, then headed to her spot behind the kitchen counter, setting up that perfect barrier between them. "What's up?"

As if deliberately encroaching on her force field, he leaned on the counter, arms outstretched, hands clasped. "I know it's Saturday, and technically it's your day off, but the kids have requested your presence at breakfast this morning."

"Oh." Sucking in a breath, she took a step back. "Gee . . . umm . . ." How could she bow out without hurting feelings? "I'm sorry, but my sister's wedding—"

"Is tomorrow. I know."

"You do?"

He smirked. "Have you forgotten what I do for a living? The wedding of Dr. Jeff and April Raine has been the topic on all the talk shows for more than a month now. Including mine."

Overcome with nervous shudders, her knees nearly collapsed. "Oh, God." Why hadn't she thought about the public scrutiny on this event before now? No wonder April had asked *her* to handle the details. Talk about pressure. Too focused on the minutiae, Summer had lost sight of the big picture.

"Don't worry. I can't speak for any of the other talk show hosts out there, but I haven't said anything mean." He looked down at the floor for a moment, then up into her face, his expression solemn. "I owe you that much."

Yes, he did. But . . .

She shook her head, took a thoughtful sip of coffee to calm her jangling nerves. "No, that's not what has me upset. Although I do appreciate that you're not maligning my family on a daily basis."

"Mind you, I have no control over what my listeners say."

She sighed. "I know. I get that. And I think that's at the core of what really scares me. Not just *your* listeners, but all those daytime viewers and the rest of the press. I guess it's finally hitting me. This wedding is a Big Deal."

He pushed away from the counter, strode around to where she stood. "So what? You're like the maid of honor or something, right?"

Too close. He stood too close to her now. Her heartbeat ramped up to overdrive, and her stomach flip-flopped. She took another step back and bumped into the oven door. To regain some kind of inner harmony, she fussed with the dish towel that hung from the oven's handle. "I'm a bridesmaid."

"Even better. Less responsibility."

"I'm also the wedding planner."

His eyes bugged. "Wow. Nanny, housekeeper, bridesmaid, wedding planner. When do you sleep?"

She exhaled a short, shaky laugh. "I know. It sounds crazy. But that's why I can't spend time with the kids today. I've gotta hit the ground running if I plan to have every detail in place for tomorrow. Would you tell them I'm sorry and that I'll see them on Monday morning? I'm most likely gonna be AWOL till then."

He took her hand in his, and warmth zapped her bloodstream. "No dice. Aren't you the one who insists they have breakfast every morning? Don't be a hypocrite. You have to eat too." He tugged her toward him.

Digging in her heels, she tugged back. "Honestly, I don't have time." And arguing with him had already put her behind schedule.

"What if we help you?"

"Help me? How?" She stopped tugging.

He didn't. Forward momentum had her colliding into his chest. His arm wrapped around her waist. "Easy there, kiddo. Don't go throwing yourself at my feet. Such a small gesture on my part doesn't deserve these kinds of accolades."

His heartbeat played on her rib cage, a symphony of promises she couldn't ignore. Last night's commentary from her sister echoed in her head. *I'd be willing to bet something else besides being needed makes you want to stay with your family, snookums.* It couldn't be true, could it? She couldn't be falling for her boss.

Clearing the sudden lump in her throat, she backed out of his hold and out of reach. *Focus, Summer.* "What exactly are you offering to do for me?"

"You tell me. I'm a man with a van, three kids, a dad, and a dog at your disposal. There must be something we can do for you. Pickup, delivery, gorilla-heavy lifting for me and Nate. Scott and Dad can do busywork that keeps them here and quiet. Maddie can color. Or sing. Or pick flowers for you. Brandy . . . well, Brandy can bark and chase her tail. And get dog hair all over you, if you're so inclined."

Despite her attempts to remain unmoved, a snicker of amusement escaped. This man could charm her into stupidity. She hid her smile behind her coffee cup and took another sip. "Hmm. I might want to skip the dog hair, thanks. The rest? Maybe. Maybe not."

"We'll be yours all day." He wheedled with the tone of a game show host enticing a contestant to sacrifice the trip to Aruba for the secret prize behind the curtain. "You can order us around any way you see fit. You just have to come down to breakfast first."

She struck a thoughtful pose, sipped more coffee. "Tempting."

"Which part? The ordering around or the breakfast?"

"A little of both."

"Good. Then meet us downstairs." His smile wide, he turned and strode away, tossing over his shoulder as he walked out, "Five minutes."

When Summer entered the kitchen about fifteen minutes later, the family stood up and shouted as one. "Surprise!"

The table was set with china, and a glass bowl full of haphazard tiger lilies and dandelions graced the center. On one side, a plate piled high with French toast sat beside a platter of bacon and a bottle of maple syrup.

"In your honor," Craig said as he took her hand to lead her farther into the room. "We used whole-wheat bread and egg substitute for the French toast, and that's turkey bacon. The maple syrup, however, is real." Through his teeth, he added, "Don't tell the food police."

"I helped Dad make the French toast," Scott boasted from his seat at the table.

"Big deal," Nate, across from Scott, scoffed. "Dad put the ingredients in front of you, and you mixed them in the bowl. It's not like you did anything *physical*." He puffed out his skinny chest. "I set the table."

"I picked the flowers," Maddie chirped. She wriggled in her booster seat and pointed to the bowl in the center of the table.

"I was the foreman on the project," Ken chimed in.

Summer's attention veered between the speakers until her head swam. "Did I miss something? What's the occasion?"

Craig leaned toward her ear. "*You*."

She turned to face him, nearly blinded by the smile on his face. "I-I don't understand."

"The kids wanted to say thank you for everything: the way the house looks, the meals, the times you took them to practices or games—"

"And when you let me wear my Minnie dress," Maddie added.

"Yeah," Craig said on a chuckle. "We don't want to forget that special occasion. Therefore, for Maddie's Minnie dress and hopscotch lessons, for keeping a cool head when Scott was injured at baseball, for standing in the rain so Nate could participate in football practice, for repairing the gutters, for transporting Brandy to the vet and suffering with all the dog hair, for transforming chaos into a haven for all of us, we present you with the first annual Hartmann Family Thank-You Breakfast."

Happiness rippled over her skin, and she practically melted into the floor. They'd done all this for her? "I'm stunned. This is such a nice surprise. Thank you."

"No," Craig said, drawing her to his seat at the table. "Thank *you*. Now eat up. You have a crazy weekend ahead. And for now, *we're* going to take care of *you*."

The craziest thought popped into Summer's head, a wish that Craig really would take care of her. In exchange, she'd gladly continue to take care of him. And his family.

Lyn paced in April's den, glancing out the window at the rain-soaked street every thirty seconds for any sign of Doug's car.

"Are you sure you don't want to ride with us?" April asked from behind her. "I still say it's pretty silly to have Doug drive all the way out here and then backtrack to the restaurant."

Shrugging into his raincoat in the foyer, Jeff remarked, "Considering we already have four in our car, I think it's rather handy to have Doug pick up Lyn." He turned to call up the stairs. "Becky? Mike? Let's get going."

Already antsy with thoughts of the discussion she planned to have with Doug, Lyn couldn't stand still.

"Do you want to back out, Lynnie?" April asked, an ocean of maternal concern. "The idea of all the reporters bothering you? Because if you can't do this, just say so. You and Doug can sit out the wedding. I swear, I won't be angry or upset. I'll understand. Really."

Sweet, tenderhearted April, always concerned about the welfare of others. With an indulgent sigh, Lyn turned away from the window and placed a hand on her sister's shoulder. "No, I'm fine. Honest. And a thousand rabid reporters wouldn't make me miss being a part of tomorrow."

"April? Sweetheart?" Jeff stepped into the room, drew April toward the door. "We should get going. Doug's probably stuck in traffic. The weather's atrocious. And since we're the hosts of tonight's soiree, we should get to the restaurant earlier than everyone else."

"Ha," April replied. "I'll bet you ten bucks Summer's already there, whipping the kitchen staff into shape."

Despite her anxiety about tonight, Lyn laughed. "I'll take that bet. After her appearance last night, I think we're seeing the beginnings of a new Summer. Someone who's not perfect, someone with flaws and interesting chinks in her armor."

"And mud on her skirt," April added.

"Mud? Summer? *Our* Summer?" Jeff interjected with a grin. "What exactly did I miss last night?"

April shook her head. "I'll tell you later. Lyn, if you're sure you'll be all right . . . ?"

"Of course. Go. Doug and I will be there in a little while." And hopefully they'd have a happy announcement of their own to make.

While April grabbed her coat from the closet, Jeff gave Lyn a wink and mouthed, *Good luck.*

Fingers crossed, she mouthed back, *Thank you.*

On thunderous thumps, Michael stomped down the staircase.

"Where's your sister?" April asked him.

"Locked in the bathroom," he replied. "As usual."

April sighed and turned to Jeff. "Go start the car. I'll get Becky."

A few minutes later, April finally herded Becky out of the house. Alone, Lyn continued to pace ruts into the carpet. When headlights flashed through the window and illuminated the wall behind her, she stopped. She took a deep breath, smoothed the creases in her skirt, and walked as sedately as her knocking knees would allow to the front door.

Doug reached the porch and stepped inside. "There's my beautiful lady," he said with a smile. "God, I missed you this last week."

His kiss left her breathless. The butterflies disappeared, replaced with the certainty of what she was about to do. "Come inside," she said. "I want to ask you something."

"Umm . . ." He looked around, his expression uneasy. "Can it wait? I wanted to take a quick detour before we went to the restaurant."

"No." The word came out too soft, too hesitant. She fisted her hands and tried again. "No," she said more forcefully. "It can't wait."

"Okay." He took a few steps away from the door, then stopped. "Where to?"

"Den." She pointed the way and followed him in. "Have a seat."

He spun, pointing from couch to club chairs to the matching hassock near the hearth. "Anywhere?"

Frustration and anxiety formed a ball in her stomach. "Sit on the couch," she bit off.

His eyes widened, and the humor left his face. "All right," he said. But he didn't sit. Instead, he closed the gap between them, and skimmed his fingers down her cheek. "What's wrong, Lyn?"

"Nothing."

"You can fool your sister, honey, but you can't fool me. Tell me what's bothering you. You're not second-guessing tomorrow, are you?"

Oh, for crying out loud! Did *everyone* think she was still afraid of her own shadow? "Of course not. I missed you, that's all."

His fingers danced down her bare arm, rippling pleasure in their wake. "I missed you too."

Another deep breath and slow exhale. "And I've been thinking."

"Yes?" His lips brushed her earlobe.

"I've been thinking it's time we talked about something permanent."

"Mmm? What kind of permanent?"

She took a step away from him, away from the delicious shivers his touch engendered. "I'm asking you to marry me, Doug."

"You're kidding."

His reaction nearly destroyed her. But somehow she managed to remain upright, despite the pain in her heart and the tears welling in her eyes. "No, I'm not kidding. But obviously I made a mistake." She turned to stare out the window, where raindrops streamed down the glass, a perfect metaphor for the emotion struggling to escape her rapidly deteriorating composure.

He had the nerve to laugh at her, and at the first chuckle, misery turned to anger. Hot, white, and fortifying. "This isn't funny, Doug."

His arm wrapped around her. "Yes, it is."

"If you think my hurt feelings are some kind of colossal joke for your enjoyment—"

"Lyn." His tone grew tender and stone-cold serious. "Look down."

She dropped her gaze from the window to his hand. Between his fingers perched a perfect pear-shaped diamond in a delicately etched golden ring.

"I planned to give this to you later. Originally, it was supposed to be during a spectacular fireworks display that distracted the rest of April and Jeff's guests. I wanted something simpler, but Summer insisted. Luckily, the heavy rain washed away her plan. That detour I wanted to take? I was going to bring you to Bald Hill and ask you there. I didn't expect you to steal my thunder."

"Bald Hill?" The war memorial? "Why on earth would you bring me to Bald Hill?"

"It's the highest point on the Island. Closest I could get to a mountain, if I didn't want to wait for winter to ask you on the bunny slope at Mount Elsie where we met. That was my original plan. But I couldn't bear to come home one more time to a place that doesn't have you in it. Vermont or Manhattan doesn't matter. Home's not home when you're not with me." With his hands on her shoulders, he turned her around, then dropped to one knee. He held the ring out to her. "Marry me, Lyn. You've already become the best thing that ever happened to me. Now I'm asking you to become the best part of me."

Joy consumed her, and she shouted her reply louder than the pounding rain. "Yes!"

Chapter Twenty

After a miserable, rainy week, April and Jeff's wedding day dawned clear, bright and, for late August on Long Island, cool. Clearly, the cosmos smiled on this happy union. Either that, or April was right. Summer had more control over the universe than she realized.

As she looked out over the grounds of The Hermitage from the third-floor balcony, Summer allowed a brief moment of smug pride to overtake her. The estate, once the crown jewel of the elusive Gold Coast, where the Vanderbilts hobnobbed with the Carnegies on Long Island's North Shore, now managed to pay its exorbitant property taxes as a catering facility and movie locale.

From the Juliet balcony, Summer had a perfect bird's-eye view of the manicured lawns and the frenetic activity below. Pink rose petals scattered across the top of the twin reflective pools in the center of the lush, English gardens. Swaths of silk, in lavender and gold, draped Greek columns spaced along the white runner, where the bride would walk to her groom. Jeff would wait for his bride beneath a white and gold pergola entwined with ivy and riotous blooms of bougainvillea.

Below the silken wings of the columns, dozens of golden urns crammed with cascades of flowers framed strategic intervals along the perimeter. A burst of color—violet, scarlet, and tangerine—enhanced the dreamy hues of the silk.

Beside her, April sighed. "It's perfect."

Yeah. It *would be* perfect. In another hour or two. Summer

still had a thousand details to attend to before the actual event, but she had outdone herself so far.

"Let's go, April." She turned away from the balcony, clapped rapidly. "Hair and makeup in the next room."

April's frown etched wrinkles in her forehead and around her lips. "You sure I can't stay here with you a little longer?"

"You having second thoughts?"

"About getting married?" She shook her head emphatically. "No way. About having the crew from *Taking Sides* broadcasting the ceremony live on the air for their nationwide audience? Ho, yeah! I'm terrified something monumentally 'April Screwup' will happen in front of the cameras. What if I trip walking down the aisle? What if a bee stings me right under the eye? What if—"

"What if you leave those pesky details to me? You know, I spent hours online last night looking for a Bette Davis quote for you." April had a habit of quoting fifties' movie stars when her emotions ran high, Bette Davis chief among them. "But apparently that old broad had a cynical view toward marriage. So I'm going to quote Judy Garland instead. 'For it was not into my ear you whispered, but into my heart. It was not my lips you kissed, but my soul.'"

April visibly relaxed, and her smile beamed brighter than the sun outside. "That's beautiful, Sum."

"So are you. Now, go on. This is your day. Yours and Jeff's. Enjoy every minute of it."

April's gaze dropped to her stocking feet. "We should have just eloped to Bermuda."

Summer grabbed her sister's hands and held them tight within her grasp. "Now, you listen to me. Your first wedding was a quickie, hush-hush affair, thanks to a surprise that became my favorite niece."

"Your *only* niece," April amended with a quirked eyebrow.

Exhaling a puff of air from pursed lips, Summer waved a dismissive hand. "Semantics. Besides, you and Jeff have found love. *Real* love. Do you have any idea how rare that is? How extraordinary? Forget the cameras, forget the people watching here and at home. When you get to the edge of the bridal runner, you focus on Jeff. Every step on that strip of white satin will take you that much closer to him, to the future you've planned together. Think of what a great dad he'll be for Becky and Mike. And maybe . . . who knows? Another kid or two?"

April blushed scarlet and yanked her hands away. "Summer!"

"What? It's not too late, is it?"

"Well, no, but . . ." She shook her head. "I've got a twenty-two-year-old daughter."

"Becky won't be twenty-two for a few months yet. And anyway, so what? That means you've got a built-in baby-sitter."

"No, it doesn't. Becs has her own life to lead, and I won't saddle her down. Time enough for her to worry about diapers and formula and overdue bills."

Oh, no. They were not going to traipse down the memory lane of April's first marriage today. Today was about joy, love, and a golden future. "Well, then you'll have to get Rainey-Day-Wife to help you out. I happen to know the owner, if you need a referral."

April placed her hands over her ears. "No office talk to-day, please. It's my wedding day."

"That's my bride. Now scoot. I've got work to do."

April turned to walk away, then whirled and hugged Summer tight enough to fracture her spine. "There's still time for you too, you know."

In a flash, Summer's imagination brought up a vision of Craig, the smile on his face yesterday when she'd fallen into his arms in her kitchen, the pulse of his heartbeat against her. She indulged the moment for a breath or two, then shook the memory away.

No. Her happiness ship had sailed long ago. Now all she had left were the splintered pieces that had dashed on the rocks of reality.

* * *

Hours later, Summer glided down the bridal runner with one of Jeff's friends as her usher. She wore a one-shouldered silken gown the color of burnished gold, and her hair was loosely twisted to the side of her nape in a low bun, lending her the aura of a Grecian goddess.

On either side of the aisle, cameras—from small personal digital units to shoulder-top video-style—held by the guests, appeared to capture every step she took. Outside the seated crowd, television cameras on wheeled dollies kept in perfect step with her and her escort.

Her hands tightened on her bouquet of pink calla and star-gazer lilies. The heat of all those klieg lights, the intense scrutiny, the *mania* had Summer itching to run away, to hide in her nice, quiet bathtub at home. No wonder Lyn hated the spotlight. Suddenly self-conscious about every breath, Summer had to force herself to move slowly, to smile, to suppress the nerves jumping synapses like some anatomical game of leapfrog. When she and her groomsman reached the pergola, she moved to the left and turned to watch the rest of the procession.

Lyn, escorted by her now fiancé, Doug, never flinched at the assortment of flashing lights and cameras. Garbed in a gown of the same golden color, hers wrapped in a more modern style, with straps on both shoulders and a sash across her waist, she glowed. Her shoulder-length hair, pulled back into an elegant chignon, perfectly framed the sparkle in her eyes. Probably a combination of happiness for April and bliss at the promise of a happily-ever-after ahead for her and Doug.

Next came Lauren with another usher. Her version of the gown had no straps, and the sashes tied in a bow at the small of her back. For her, the hairstylist had created a chignon out of two French braids, a slight departure from Lyn's more classic hairdo.

The tuxes looked great on all the guys, the ivory shirts against the black jackets and black ties just the right contrast to the bridesmaids' gowns. And really, Summer thought as she scanned the men, from Jeff all the way down the line, nobody cared what they wore anyway. No guest ever left a wedding with the comment, "Didn't the groom look fabulous in his tuxedo?" Except maybe his mother.

For everyone else, today was all about the bride and bridesmaids. The gowns, the flowers, the hairstyles all piqued the crowd's interest.

And the love. Weddings were always about the love.

Becky, as maid of honor, was the last attendant to walk the runner, hers a solo appearance. Her gown tied halterstyle with the sash draped to one side, ending in a rosette on her hip. She wore her hair in a low side ponytail, a wisp of bangs swept over one eye. The four of them looked different enough to reflect their varied ages and personalities, yet still cohesive enough to be part of the same bridal party.

Once Becky had reached the end of the runner, an expectant hush fell over the crowd. The orchestra, seated behind the guests at the rear of the grounds, broke into a heartmelting instrumental rendition of the old Elvis classic "Can't Help Falling in Love."

April appeared on the arm of her son Michael. Unlike with the other males, the tuxedo transformed Michael into an entirely different individual than the awkward teen everyone expected. He stood taller, his expression solemn, doe eyes fixed straight ahead, almost like a stern father. Yet, the twitch of his lips hinted at a struggle to hide his pride at playing such an important part in this ceremony.

As he led April slowly forward, the blazing television lights sparkled the beading and crystals on the bodice of her pale pink satin gown. The mid-afternoon sun added an extra glow to her bare shoulders. More of the crystals, appliquéd into falling diamonds, embellished the slightly belled ballerina skirt and winked with every step of her rhinestonestudded, ivory high-heeled sandals.

She'd eschewed a veil in favor of a simple pink and ivory crystal headpiece of geometric shapes. Her short chestnut hair had been curled with hot rollers, then swept into a sassy updo. She was beautiful, ageless, timeless. The perfect bride with an updated twist.

Her Biedermeier-styled bouquet contained a circle of pink roses, surrounded by a circle of yellow roses, all interspersed with snowy stephanotis and white cymbidium orchids. Simple, stunning, and the ideal complement to all the gowns.

Summer stole a glance at Jeff to gauge his reaction at the first sight of his bride. The love shining in his eyes confirmed her belief in happily-ever-after. Warmth infused her, and she sighed with contentment. She'd made this happen for them. At last, she'd done something for April that would atone for all the years she'd stolen her toys, poked fun at her misery, and acted like the supreme Wicked Witch of the West.

"Amazing," Lyn whispered to her. "Everything is absolutely perfect, Sum. You're going to have to work hard to top this for Doug and me."

Summer smiled. "Piece of cake, Lyn," she whispered back. "I already have some great ideas in mind for you."

"Well, then, I humbly bow to the expert."

Oh, no doubt about it. Summer *was* an expert at controlling other peoples' lives. She just couldn't seem to keep her own on track.

Craig stared at the television screen—more precisely, at Summer, who stood in the crowd on the side of the dance floor. The camera zoomed in on the bride and groom, but Craig's attention remained riveted to the smaller image of Summer, a smiling face in a throng of smiling faces.

"Summer looks pretty," his father remarked from the recliner in the corner.

Pretty? Craig stifled a snort of impatience. If ever a word didn't do a woman justice, *pretty* for how Summer looked right now reigned supreme. She glowed in gold, brighter than the goddess of the sun. He frowned as he continued to stare at her. Why wasn't she on the dance floor?

"Don't you think she looks pretty, Maddie?" Dad continued.

"Uh-huh. Daddy, can I have a dress like Summer's?"

He didn't answer, barely heard the question as he stared at Summer, at her smile, the exotic fall of her hair to her bare shoulder, the sparkle in her eyes. So incredibly beautiful. Why was she all alone?

"Earth to Craig!" Dad shouted.

"Huh?" He snapped back to reality. "Oh, umm . . . I don't know, sweetheart. Maybe when you're older, okay?"

"Dad?" Scott asked. "Can I have a monster truck like Bigfoot?"

"Yeah, sure, I guess," he replied absentmindedly.

"That does it." Dad sat up, shoved the recliner's footrest closed, then stood. "Come on, Craig. Let's go figure out what's for dinner."

Gaze never leaving the screen, he waved off his dad. "I'll just order in."

Dad's hand clamped his shoulder. "No. Summer would have a fit if you fell back on old habits. Especially when we have the time and the ingredients to do better." His voice hummed low in Craig's ear. "Get up, son. We need to talk. Alone. Unless you want your kids to hear your old man giving you a lecture about the birds and the bees."

Craig finally broke the trance of the televised wedding and turned to glare at his father. "I don't need a lecture, Dad."

"Yeah, you do. Get up. Now."

With the resentment of an angsty teen, Craig shot to his feet and clumped his way from the living room to the kitchen. Reaching the sink, he whirled and growled, "What in shinola are you rambling about, Dad? Can't you see I'm in the middle of something?"

"Oh, you're in the middle of something, all right." Dad folded his arms over his chest. "You're up to your ears in love, son."

He gripped the counter behind him until his knuckles ached. "That's the dumbest thing I've ever heard. I'm not in love with Summer. She's an employee."

Dad's raucous laughter stiffened Craig's spine. "*That's* the dumbest thing *I've* ever heard." Sobering, he shook his head. "You may have gone to that Rainey Day place looking to hire an employee, but you wound up with a woman who fills this whole house with light and laughter. And unlike Chelsea, who wanted the celebrity rather than the substance, Summer sees the real you. Thank God."

Craig scrubbed a hand across his chin. Maureen had said something similar, something about him showing his real self to Summer. So what? He couldn't exactly hide himself or his kids from the woman hired to take care of all of them.

"Come on, Craig," Dad continued. "There's no shame in admitting you've got a thing for Summer. Heck, I'd have a thing for her if I were twenty years younger with a stronger heart. You've been alone a long time. And you couldn't fall for a better woman than Summer. She's beautiful and smart—"

"And just about perfect," Craig added with a solemn head shake.

"Nobody's perfect, Craig."

"Which is why I said she's *just about* perfect, Dad." He pushed away from the counter, ran a hand through his hair. "Wanna know how I know she's not perfect? She's still hooked on her ex-husband, that's why. You should have seen her the other day when we ran into him at the hardware store. Trust me. She's not interested in a romance with a bum like me."

Dad shrugged. "Well, okay, I didn't see her at the hardware store, but I've seen her every day since she first got here. And in case you haven't noticed, which I suspect you haven't, since you obviously spend most of your time coming up with excuses why she's not interested in a bum like you, Summer's *very much* interested in you too."

"Bull."

"Fact. Anyone with decent eyesight can see the way she looks at you, the way you look at her. For God's sake, I have cataracts and I'm practically blinded from the sparks between you two." He planted a hand on the countertop. "Ask her out to dinner, share some time with her that has nothing to do with me and the kids. Tell her how you feel. The worst that could happen is she turns you down and the atmosphere gets a little awkward around here for a while."

"Great," he muttered. "Just what I need with Chelsea breathing down my neck."

"Chelsea's *always* breathing down your neck. Don't let her scare you into sacrificing your happiness. Life's too short."

Chapter Twenty-one

After nearly an hour of watching happy couples dance—Jeff and April, Lyn and Doug, Lauren and an exotic-looking piece of eye candy named Elijah, even Becky with that Ace Riordan character—Summer's single status burned like a brand. She told herself she was better off without a date; she already had too many demands on her time here. But as the couples swept over the dance floor, regret stabbed her. She should have asked Craig to come with her. He would have made her laugh, helped her with the details, and not felt put out when she disappeared for several minutes to handle a crisis.

When she finally couldn't take the discomfort any longer, she ducked into the observatory hall for some alone time. Of course, if anyone asked, she was there to cool off and check on the dessert table. Well worth the stop, in her modest opinion. Picturing the sweet assortments from a photographer's point of view, she smiled with pride. Delicious *and* artistic.

Gold-rimmed plates of bone china held cannoli stuffed with chocolate pistachio cream, decadent dark chocolate truffles drizzled with raspberry sauce, slices of orange rum cake, pear frangipane, and praline bars. A dozen flavors of cheesecake were perched on sticks, lollipops for adult palates. Strawberries wore white chocolate "gowns" or dark chocolate "tuxedos." At center stage in the middle of this caloric cornucopia stood the wedding cake, a tower of four gold squares that looked beautiful enough to wear as jewelry, studded with lifelike—but fully edible—calla and stargazer lilies. Sheer perfection at every angle.

A slender arm wrapped around her waist, and a voice whispered in her ear. "Boo!"

On a stifled gasp, she whirled.

"Easy, Aunt Summer. It's just me." Becky grinned at her. "Mom and Dad want you outside. Now."

"Dad?" Last she heard, both kids called Jeff by his name—when they bothered to address him at all.

"Yeah, well, it's official now. He's family. I've been thinking of him as 'Dad' for a while, but I knew how much it meant to Mom for me to say it. So . . ." She shifted her weight to one hip, hands outstretched, palms up. "That's my wedding present to the happy couple."

Summer couldn't help but smile at Becky's insight. "Clever girl. That should make your mother deliriously happy."

"And"—Becky bobbed her head from side to side—"it doesn't cost me anything."

"Yeah, it does, sweetheart. The cost isn't financial, it's emotional. And that makes the gesture even more precious." She pulled her niece into a tight embrace. "And your mom is going to weep like a baby when she hears you say it the first time, so do me a favor. Make sure you wait till the cameras are gone."

"Too late," she replied cheekily. "But don't worry. We fixed her face in the ladies' room a few minutes ago. She still looks perfect. Now come on. Everybody's waiting."

Becky grabbed her hand and took off at a run that forced Summer to keep up or risk being dragged on her chest from the observatory to the gardens. She finally stopped at the front of the dance floor, a portable black-and-white checkerboard laid out near the twin reflecting pools. "Got her, Mom and *Dad*," she announced, while Summer wheezed, catching her breath.

Standing with Jeff on the raised dais where the orchestra played a slow dance number, April beamed. "Thanks, Becs." She took the microphone in hand and waited until the strains of the song played out. "Ladies and gentlemen," she said at last, "Jeff and I want to thank each of you for joining us today. As most of you might already know, I placed all the details and planning of this wedding into two very capable hands. My sister Summer Raine pulled off what I would have definitely screwed up." She laughed and waved away the groans and denials of the audience. "And I want to take this opportunity to thank Summer for giving me"—she looked at Jeff and beamed—"for giving *us* the perfect wedding."

Applause burst from the crowd. And over the thunderous hoots and clapping, she added in a much louder voice, "If Summer decided to create a new career for herself, she'd make the ideal wedding planner. I can tell you from personal experience, any bride would be lucky to have her expertise."

Summer's jaw dropped.

On the dais, Jeff handed April a flute of champagne. Lifting another filled flute in the air, he toasted, "To Summer. Thank you!"

Glasses of all shapes, filled with a variety of liquors, popped up around Summer. After April sipped, so did Jeff, then everyone else. Nodding to the orchestra leader, April took Jeff's hand, and they descended the few stairs leading off the platform. Meanwhile, the band broke into a rendition of Glenn Miller's "In the Mood." Dozens of couples headed for the dance floor.

Once April hit solid ground, Summer wasted no time confronting her older sister. "How did you know?"

April, aglow with newlywed happiness, laughed. "Have you forgotten how nosy I am? You left notes scattered all over your desk at the office. I admit, I looked because I thought they were about my wedding. And some were. But a lot of them were business plans, cost scenarios, and even cutesy wedding names you were considering. And honestly, Summer? I think you've found your calling. You're *really* good. Today has been more perfect than I could have ever dreamed."

She practically preened at the praise. "I'm glad. I wanted today to be special for you."

"Special? It's been *amazing*. When I think about all the stuff going on in your personal life through most of my wedding plans—your divorce, Brad kicking you out of the house, working with the man who destroyed your marriage—God, Summer, you created magic today. If you could do so much for me, imagine what you could do for someone when you don't have all the distractions!" In an aside, she added, "That little announcement of mine just went out coast to coast. I bet you'll have a dozen soon-to-be brides clamoring for your attention within a week."

A thrill rippled through her. Could it really be so easy? "How can I thank you?"

April laughed. "Hell-o? You still don't get it, do you? *I'm* thanking *you,* Sum. I want you to stop hiding at the Hartmann house. Go be who you were meant to be."

Stop hiding at the Hartmann house. That quickly, the excitement froze in her veins. Was that what April thought? That she was hiding? *Was* she hiding?

Go be who you were meant to be. She thought back to yesterday: the breakfast, the way they'd all pitched in to help her get ready for today's event. Nate and Craig schlepped two hundred individually boxed and gift-wrapped packages of gourmet coffee with sterling serving scoops from the distributor's warehouse to The Hermitage. Ken sat with Scott, creating an emergency sewing kit while the boy packed a small lace bag with Band-Aids and other first-aid items. All for her, to spend time with her, to thank her, to help her.

Go be who you were meant to be. Wedding planner or Hartmann family caregiver? What if she wanted both?

Hours later, Summer crept into her apartment, flipped on the kitchen light, dropped the pastry box on the counter, and slipped out of her high-heeled, open-toed shoes. Her feet nearly sighed their relief. God, what a day! As exhausted as she felt, she knew she'd have trouble falling asleep with all the day's events playing over and over in her head.

Loneliness overwhelmed her yet again. She'd give anything

for someone to be here right now, willing to sit up and talk with her. Someone who'd listen to her crow about the successes, help her wind down from the frenetic pace she'd kept since six this morning. Maybe she should invest in a goldfish, because no one waited in her shabby den.

She'd lost track of all her neighborhood friends after the divorce. Couples dinner parties and martini get-togethers were awkward with an unattached female along for the ride. She grimaced when she considered how shallowly she'd lived her life: an endless stream of manicures, cocktails, and gossip. Nothing of substance or meaning. Until now. Look at what she'd done for Craig and his family. Their house was clean and organized. They were eating healthy meals. They had time for their games and practices. All three kids were beginning to act more responsibly and politely. Oh, they still needed guidance, but she'd wrought some miracle changes already.

And thinking of miracles brought her full circle to today. In providing April and Jeff with the wedding of their dreams, she'd contributed something memorable to their love story. She really wanted to create those memories for other blissful couples.

Maybe April was right. Maybe she should stop waiting for her life to begin. Long past time to go out and seize her happiness, no matter how it came to her.

A soft knock sounded on her door, and she jumped. Panic set in as she glanced at the clock on the microwave. 1:15 A.M. Oh, God! The kids! Did something happen to one of the kids? One hand clutched her chest to keep her pounding heart shielded as she raced to the door and opened it.

Craig blinked, eyes wide, apparently as surprised as she. Then he flashed a great big grin. "Congratulations," he whispered.

"Huh?"

"The wedding. I watched the coverage."

Her brows nearly hit her hairline. "You . . . watched my sister's wedding?"

"Still can't seem to remember what I do for a living, huh?" He leaned inside, scanned the living room/kitchen area. "Am I disturbing you? Is it okay if I come in?"

"Umm . . . yeah. Sure." Leaving the door open, she stepped back to stare at the clock again. Yes, definitely after one in the morning.

"You looked great, by the way," he said. He gave her the once-over from head to toe. "Still do. That gown. Wow. Perfect for you."

"Thanks." Could the entire human body blush? If not, she might be coming down with something. The slow heat creeping over her skin indicated either embarrassment or a fever. Even her bare feet felt too warm against the floorboards.

He stared at her, his look expectant, and she stared back. The air crackled. She fought the urge to smooth her hair, knew her hands shook too badly to carry off an image of nonchalance. Better to turn the focus of the conversation. "Craig? What are you doing up at this hour? Is everything okay?"

"Everything's fine. I heard you come in and just wanted to congratulate you. That looked like a pretty amazing party. And your sister said you planned it all?"

She blinked. "You *know* I planned it all. You helped me yesterday, remember?"

"Oh, yeah." He loitered near the kitchen counter, drawing invisible figures in the beige Formica.

What exactly was he fishing for? Didn't matter. The richest bait wouldn't get a nibble out of her right now. "Well, thanks for coming up, but I'm really wiped. You should get some sleep, and God knows I'll be out cold the minute my head hits the pillow." A total lie, but he didn't know that.

"Actually, I had a few questions about the wedding." He shot up a hand. "Not for my audience. For my own curiosity."

She cocked her head, tried to read his face, found his expression inscrutable. "Oh? Like what?"

"I wanted to ask you . . ." His gaze dropped to his feet. "How come you were alone?"

"Excuse me?"

His head shot up, eyes unblinking. "You had no date."

She felt the verbal slap, and roiled with the insult. "Gee, that was subtle."

A flush crept over his face, and he rubbed his throat. "Sorry. It's late. My subtlety went to bed hours ago."

"Then maybe you should go to bed yourself." She opened the refrigerator door, feigning interest in a cold drink when, in reality, she needed the barrier between them to protect her feelings.

"Ah, Summer, I'm sorry. Really. I'm mucking this all up. I just can't imagine why someone as beautiful as you . . ." He shook his head. "Nope. Forget it. Good night."

He turned to walk away, but Summer suddenly realized she wanted him here. She'd just finished wishing for someone to talk to when opportunity knocked on her door in the form of this man. Time to start seizing the opportunities that presented themselves. "Craig?"

He stopped.

She took a deep breath, spoke on the exhale. "I'm a little bit wired from today. Any chance I could convince you to have a seat, maybe pull an all-nighter with me?"

He didn't even take a minute to think about it. "Why not? At this point, I'm only going to get about two hours' sleep, anyway. Got anything cold to drink in that box you're hiding behind?"

The blush flourished to a bonfire. "Water? Iced tea? It's diet . . . ," she added apologetically.

"I'll take it."

"If you want some extra calories, I also have a box of pastries from the wedding."

"Anything good?"

"All of it's good. Chocolate pistachio cannoli, pear frangipane, orange rum cake."

"Stop. You had me at cannoli."

She laughed, placed the iced tea pitcher on the counter, and closed the refrigerator door with a hip. A quick detour into the freezer for an ice tray—oh, how she missed a modern appliance with a built-in icemaker—and two glasses from the cabinet. With the glasses filled, she handed him one, then pointed to the kitchen table. "Have a seat."

He plopped into a chair, and she grabbed the white cardboard box of pastries, then followed him.

"So . . ." Flipping open the box, he studied the contents. "You never did answer my question."

"What question was that?"

"Why no date?"

She sipped her tea, scrambling for something to say, and finally settled on the truth. "Originally, I would have gone with Brad."

"Ah, yes. Brad the Cad."

She pointed a finger, pistol-like. "Cute. I've never heard it put quite like that before, but, yes, now that you mention it, he was the ultimate cad. After the divorce, I cut him from the guest list."

"A wise decision."

"One of only a very few I made back then."

He winced. "You're referring to us, aren't you? Working here was one of those unwise decisions."

"No." She shook her head. At his dubious expression, she repeated more emphatically, "*No.* After I found out about Brad from . . ." She let the sentence trail off. "Well, you know how I found out."

"Yeah. I know. And I'm sorry."

"Don't. It's done. And I'm fine with it. But that night . . ." Thinking back on that evening of destruction, she smiled grimly. "I went nuts. Destroyed his clothes, set fire to his cigars, I even threatened to take a sledgehammer to his Porsche."

He nodded his approval. "Justifiable."

"Childish. And stupid. Anyway, no Brad, no date. End of story."

"Uh-huh." With his reaction bland, he picked up a cannoli, bit into the crisp shell. Only then did his expression change, momentarily, to bliss.

Dipping into the box, she pulled out a chocolate-covered

strawberry. "Besides"—she bit into the sweet fruit—"I was so busy seeing to all the wedding details, I didn't really have time for a date today. I didn't even dance."

He popped the last bite of cannoli into his mouth, then licked the powdered sugar from his fingertips. "Well, now that's a shame. Here you are, all dressed up, looking like a million bucks—did I tell you that you looked terrific, by the way? And you didn't even dance?" His gaze scanned the room. "You don't happen to have a radio or a boombox in here, do you?"

"Just the clock radio in the bedroom."

He shook his head. "No good." Rising, he held out his hand. "Come with me."

"Where?"

"You'll see."

She placed her hand in his, a tiny thrill pulsing through her veins. He led her into the living room, picked up the remote control from her coffee table and flipped on the television. The dark room burst into soft light. "What's your pleasure? A slow number? A little slam dancing? A polka?"

She treaded closer to him, closer to the energy palpable between them. "Slow, I guess."

"Perfect." He punched a few numbers on the remote, and seconds later, a rhythm and blues love ballad played out from the television. "God bless cable's music channels." Dropping the remote onto the table with a thunk, he held up a hand, palm facing her. "Ready?"

"For what?"

"For a dance. No way I'm going to allow you to let that dress go to waste."

He didn't wait for a reply. One hand wrapped her waist, and he pulled her to him. For a minute, she considered protesting, but couldn't form a logical argument. He swayed to the music. The hand on her waist brushed the silken gown against her skin, sending delicious shivers through her body. She stared up into his face, into those magnificent eyes— blue flames in the dimly lit room. He hummed the song while they danced, the rhythmic sound resonating from his chest to hers. The song changed, but the dance remained the same.

"I used to sing this to Maddie when she was teething and couldn't sleep."

"Lucky girl," she murmured.

"Lucky me, it worked. Nothing worse than walking the halls with a screaming infant and counting off the minutes of sleep you're losing."

"Oh, God." She let go and broke away. "I'm sorry. I'm keeping you up."

He pulled her back into his arms. "Yeah, you're keeping me up. In a good way. If I didn't want to be here, I wouldn't have come." He tucked her head under his chin and continued the dance. "When I saw you on TV today, standing on the sidelines, surrounded by all those couples in love, I realized I wished I'd been there to dance with you. So indulge me, okay?"

"Okay." What else could she say? Craig seemed to know exactly how to charm her into submission. And not for nothing, but she enjoyed this experience too much to insist he stop. His heartbeat kept time with hers, the silk glided over her skin, and she glowed like the fireflies Maddie loved to chase.

His thumb traced a lazy line around her ear, down her cheek, then tilted up her chin. She licked her lips, waited a breath, and closed her eyes. He must have understood her unspoken request, because his mouth touched hers. This time there was no audience, no reason for him to pretend an attraction for some ulterior motive.

She took what he offered and yearned for more. His kiss, hesitant at first, grew bolder until her toes curled.

He broke away, and she took a shaky breath.

"I shouldn't have—"

Before he could finish, she placed her fingers over his lips. "I'm glad you did. Craig, there's something between us. You feel it. God knows I feel it. And if you tell me I'm just your employee again, I might have to kick you in your kneecaps."

"You're not my employee. And you're more than a very good friend too." He drew her close again. "I wanted to deny I had feelings for you. I've been putting my life on hold for the kids' sake. Then you walked into my house. I've tried so hard to dismiss you from my mind, but apparently everyone knows how we feel about each other. I've heard lectures from friends, and even my dad."

Summer's memory cast back to the conversation with the ladies at Riff's Grill the other night. She laughed. "I got the same speech, I'm sure."

"Today, when I saw you at that wedding, looking so lonely, I had this sudden urge to drive over to The Hermitage. I wanted to stand at your side and tell everyone who'd listen how extraordinary you are."

"So why didn't you?"

"Because I figured security would toss me out on my keister before I got within inches of you."

Yes, they would have. She smiled and pressed her head to his chest. "Next time," she murmured, thinking of Lyn and Doug's wedding in the near future. "From now on, you're my date."

"Sounds a whole lot better than 'employer,' doesn't it?"

"You got that right!" she said with another laugh.

They spent the next two hours talking, dancing, and kissing. Oh, the kisses! Some were soft as desert rain, others as heady as a plunge from an airplane. Each, however, was unique and soul-shattering.

At three thirty, Craig finally gave her one last kiss. "I should go. I need to grab a shower and do some prep before work. And you should get some sleep."

Sleep. Yeah, right. As if she could. And yet, belying the tumult of jumpy emotions inside her heart and mind, she suddenly yawned.

"Go," he said. "Get some sleep."

"But that's not fair. I've kept you awake and you have to go to work."

"I've endured a lot of sleepless nights, Summer. But this is the first time I've *enjoyed* being awake all night since my college days. I'd rather stay up all night, dancing with you in this crummy apartment, than get a full eight hours' shut-eye in a five-star hotel room."

Her entire body sparkled with delight. Hard to believe this smooth, gentle man was Cliff Hanger, obnoxious jerk from the radio.

She closed her eyes, and he kissed her cheek. "Go. I'll see you later."

When she opened her eyes again, he was gone. The room was still, except for the music coming from the television. His sudden departure sapped all her energy. She sank onto the couch, and for the first time in years, didn't contemplate a single list.

Chapter Twenty-two

With sleep evading her, Summer opted to get an early start on her usual morning routine of coffee, exercise, and a shower.

After all the crazy events of yesterday, she couldn't imagine what might happen today. One thing was certain. She and Craig were about to dive into a new relationship. How would the rest of the family react? Ken probably would crow that he knew it all along. But the kids? The kids might not like this change.

Squaring her shoulders, she prepared to face the day and opened her apartment door to head downstairs. Once on the main level, she knocked on the boys' bedroom door.

Nate poked his head out. "I'm up." He stepped out into the hall in his Superman pajamas.

"Shower," she ordered gently. "Breakfast in fifteen minutes."

While the boy padded toward the bathroom, rubbing his eyes, Summer aimed for the kitchen. Since yesterday's events had thrown off her regular routine, she played with different menu items in her head so she'd know how to set the table. The weather was too humid for something heavy like pancakes. They'd had French toast on Saturday during that sweet surprise for her. Cereal was a possibility, but only with fruit and whole-grain toast on the side.

She stepped into the kitchen and stopped short. The table was set, almost as if she'd done it in her sleep last night. *Almost.* Because whoever had distributed the silverware had left a knife near Maddie's seat. A butter knife, but a knife nonetheless.

"Morning."

Summer turned to find Ken in the doorway, fully dressed, a white ceramic mug in his hand. She indicated the set table. "You did this?"

He grinned. "Guilty as charged. I figured you could use some help this morning."

"Thank you."

"You're welcome. But I can't take all the credit. Craig made dinner last night, cleaned up the kitchen afterward, packed Nate's lunch, the whole nine yards. I guess your influence is wearing off on him. I even asked him if he planned to start wearing your skirts." He scanned her from head to toe. "My son don't have your legs, though."

When he headed for the coffeemaker for a refill, she took advantage of his distraction to surreptitiously remove the knife from Maddie's reach. The family was becoming independent. Oh, they still needed help, but soon, that help wouldn't be daily. A housecleaner two or three times a week would probably suffice. September was around the corner. The boys would return to school, Maddie would start preschool, and Ken would be recovered enough to handle drop-offs and pickups at the bus stop without an issue.

So maybe she could actually turn the page, start a new chapter in her life without feeling guilty. She and Craig could transition from employer/employee to romantic couple, while she turned her wedding-planning business from fantasy to reality.

One thing April had said yesterday resonated with her. She'd managed to pull off a dream wedding, even with the type of distractions that would have devastated a weaker wedding planner. So why couldn't she continue to juggle both jobs? Wedding plans didn't get hectic in the early stages, which gave her plenty of time to ease from one job description to the other. She didn't have to leave here right away.

Mind tumbling amid her plans, she scrambled egg whites

with turkey, broccoli, and cheddar cheese for the family breakfast. As she slid the food onto the plates, her cell phone buzzed in her hip pocket. She flinched, nearly dropped the plate she held, but caught it at the last second and managed to place the omelet in front of Nate. Before the next series of buzzing commenced, she grabbed the phone and hit the connect button. "Hello?"

"What in Aunt Fanny's farm have you done to me?" a strident voice demanded.

"Brenda? Is that you?" Why on earth would April's second-in-command call at this hour?

"Yes, it's Brenda. And I need you to come down to the office. Now!"

"I'm making breakfast—"

"*Now,* Summer. As in twenty minutes ago."

"Why? What's happening?"

"What's happening is this place has gone nuclear on me, and since you're responsible, I want your help."

Summer had known Brenda for years and had never heard her sound so frantic. And what did Brenda mean that *she* was responsible? For what? Only one way to find out. "Okay. Hang on a sec." She cupped a hand over the speaker and asked Ken, "Okay if I leave Maddie and Scott with you for an hour or two after breakfast? Some kind of emergency at the office."

"Yeah, sure," he said through a mouthful of egg whites and turkey. "Whatever you need."

"Great. Thanks, Ken." She uncovered the mouthpiece. "Brenda, give me thirty minutes."

"Ten would be a whole lot better, Summer."

"I'll do the best I can, but I still have responsibilities here." Ken waved her off. "Go. I got this."

"Are you sure?"

"Go. Scoot. Skedaddle."

"I'm on my way, Brenda."

Detouring only long enough to grab her purse, she climbed into her Escalade and drove off. When she strode inside

Rainey-Day-Wife's office a short time later, she stepped into a cacophony of ringing phones. Five people sat at their desks, all already answering calls. A frazzled-looking Brenda—hair wild, eyes darting up, down, left, right—flipped the mouthpiece of her headset away from her lips and expelled an exhausted exhale. "Thank God."

Summer glanced around at the buzz of activity, the harried employees, and frowned. "What's going on?"

"What's going on? I'll tell you what's going on. I've got three dozen messages from brides all over the New York area who want to hire you. And every time I pick up the phone, another woman is demanding to know how she can get in touch with April Raine's fabulous wedding planner."

"Really?" Excitement rippled through her.

"Don't 'really' me. This is a nightmare."

She probably shouldn't smile, but Summer couldn't stifle the joy that infused her from head to toe. "Okay, I'm sorry. But what should I do? Where do I start? I mean, I'm totally unprepared—"

"For starters, get yourself a business phone. Something separate from your current cell number. Then give me the number so I can put something on our company voice mail and stem the madness here."

Brenda's phone rang again, and she disconnected the headset. "You answer this one." She pushed away from her desk. "I need more coffee."

Summer reached across to pick up the receiver and deliver the usual spiel. "Thank you for calling Rainey-Day-Wife. How can I make your burden easier today?"

"Good morning," a clipped, heavily British voice said on the other end of the phone. "It *is* morning there, right? I always get the time zones screwed up."

Easing into the chair beside the desk, Summer smiled. "Yes, it's morning here. May I help you?"

"I certainly hope so. My name is Daphne Beech. I'm the personal assistant for Duchess DeeLight."

Duchess DeeLight? The international pop star? No way.

This was a prank. Still, professional courtesy insisted she play along until the game ended with a bunch of teenage giggles and a hang up. "How can I help you today, Ms. Beech?"

"I'm looking for Summer Raine, the wedding planner."

"Lucky you. You found her."

"Answering your own phone? How . . . *American* of you." While the tone was complimentary, the emphasis she placed on that one word got Summer's back up. Before she could form a biting reply, the woman pressed on. "May I ask for some kind of proof you are who you say you are?"

"I might ask the same of you, Ms. Beech."

High-pitched laughter trilled from the receiver. "You might, indeed. I suppose we'll simply have to trust that each of us is who we say we are. But if word of our conversation leaks to the American press, I'll hold Summer personally responsible, whether or not you're her."

Summer frowned. Hardly seemed fair. "Why don't you tell me exactly why you called, and we'll take it from there?"

"Mmm," the woman replied. "Suspicious. I approve. I'd like to sit down with you in person to discuss a business venture. I can be in New York on Thursday if that meets with your approval. Say . . . two o'clock at the Palm Court in the Plaza Hotel?"

"Can we make it three instead?" She'd already inconvenienced Ken enough with today's flight from the house. But with enough notice, she could make sure Craig was home in time to stay with the kids on Thursday.

"Three o'clock? Perfect. We'll do their afternoon tea."

Brenda returned with her coffee mug, hovered near the desk, curiosity brewing in her tired eyes.

Meanwhile, Summer grabbed a pen and a yellow sticky pad and scrawled down the details: *Daphne Beech, asst. for Duchess DeeLight, Palm Court, 3 p.m., Thursday.*

Brenda's eyes went buggy as she read along. "*The* Duchess DeeLight?" she mouthed to Summer.

Summer shrugged. "I'll be there," she said into the phone.

"Splendid. Thank you so much, Summer. I'll make the

reservations under my name. I'm looking forward to meet-ing you. Cheers."

"Umm . . . yeah. Cheers." She hung up, stared at the phone as if she expected someone to pop out of the little black box and scream, "Gotcha!"

"Duchess DeeLight?" Brenda asked again as she sank into her chair behind the desk. "Seriously?"

Summer turned to face her. "I don't know. The woman *says* she works for the singer, but this could be some idiot's idea of a joke. Or a potential bride who figures she'll drop a famous name to get me to give her priority. I honestly don't know."

"Or it could be legit."

Legit. Her brain immediately started making a mental list of pros and cons.

Pro: *If this Beech woman really wanted her to plan a wedding for the hottest music sensation to come from England since the Beatles, her business would get worldwide publicity.*

Con: *Provided the wedding was a hit. If the bride wasn't happy, the backlash could destroy her reputation in the field.*

Pro: *Money wouldn't be an issue, so there'd be no finan-cial limit on what her imagination could dream up. The most impressive venue, designer fashions, Faberge wedding favors, nothing was out of the realm of possibility.*

Con: *A diva like Duchess DeeLight could be demand-ing and nearly impossible to please.*

Pro: *Rubbing elbows with rich and famous celebrities who might, in turn, require her services for them-selves or a family member. That kind of fame could launch her without an expensive advertising budget.*

Con: *A lot less time with Craig. And Ken. And the kids.*

Her enthusiasm evaporated. "I think I'd rather start out small," she murmured.

Brenda patted her hand. "Wedding jitters. And not only are you *not* the bride, you don't even have the gig yet." A quick squeeze to Summer's fingertips. "Get that business phone for now. Field some other calls. Make no decisions until you've really thought about what you want and where you want to take this, okay? And don't forget your *other* sister just got engaged. She's going to want your help too."

Of course! Lyn and Doug! Lyn had even asked for Summer's help planning their nuptials during the reception yesterday. And she really did have some interesting ideas in mind for those two.

So for now, she'd take Brenda's advice. First stop, her cellular distributor for a business account. And of course, she'd need a name for her company. She had a list of possibilities in her apartment, from the pun *Raine or Shine Bride* to the pedestrian *Weddings by Summer* to the snarky tag April had given her wedding to Brad a decade ago, *Summer's Splendiferous Spousal Spectaculars*.

Okay, that last one was more a joke than a serious contender. But apparently she had no more time for jokes. Her business had just taken off. She thought about last night with Craig. In some strange quirk of fate, simultaneously, her love life had decided to revive itself.

She was seriously going to have to buckle up for this ride.

When Craig arrived home that afternoon, Summer came running at top speed from the front door.

She threw herself at him, practically sucking the breath from his lungs when she collided with him. Flinging her arms around his neck, she breathed heavily into his ear. "You are *not* going to believe the day I had today."

"Easy, hon," he murmured. "I need to break this thing between us to the kids slowly."

"I know. I'm sorry." She stepped back, but the smile playing on her lips was far from apologetic.

"Okay. What am I missing?"

He tried to keep up. Really, he did. But the words spilled

out of her at such a rapid pace, he only caught random phrases. He had to rely on his already exhausted brain to piece together the gist of her conversation. Best as he could decipher, she planned to start some kind of wedding business, and April had somehow made her services popular overnight. There was some talk in there about the pop star Duchess DeeLight, high tea at the Palm Court, a bunch of ringing telephones, and someone named Brenda. None of what she said made a lot of sense, but her excitement charged the atmosphere like an electrical storm.

"Isn'tthatthemostincrediblethingever?" she summed up.

He gave up trying to wend his way through the entire wilderness and opted to bluff for now. "Incredible. How about we go inside and talk about it in more detail?"

"Okay." She practically skipped toward the house, and he followed behind, a tired smile quirking his lips. Whatever happened today had replaced the lovely, serious child-care provider with this delightful waif. Apparently, his Summer had as many moods as the season she was named for: sunny, breezy, stormy, balmy, hot, and now playful.

He stopped in the middle of the walkway, thought about how he'd just referred to her. *His* Summer. He shook his head. Weird. Recalling that fateful day in the studio when he'd decided to take advantage of a random phone call that might entertain his audience, he had to laugh. If Maureen—or anyone else for that matter—had predicted that six months later, the innocent victim of his stunt would not only be living under his roof, but having him falling in love again, he would have ordered a battery of psychological tests.

Go figure. Maybe the old pundits were right. Sometimes, truth *was* stranger than fiction.

Ahead of him, the subject of his musings halted, turned, stamped a foot, then raced back to grab his hand. "Come on! Scott's playing video games, your dad's taken Maddie to the playground, and we've got fifteen minutes, tops, before Nate's bus gets here. I have so much to tell you."

Still?

"Summer, slow down. Please. I've been awake for more than thirty-three hours at this point."

"So have I. But let's see if I can rejuvenate you a little." She zoomed in, planted a kiss on his mouth that left him breathless. *Rejuvenated,* but breathless. "Better?"

He wrapped an arm around her waist to pull her closer. "Not yet, but getting there."

Behind them, a car door slammed. "Gee, Craig. I hope I'm not interrupting anything."

Her familiar voice slinked down his spine like a rat's tail, and he stiffened. "Chelsea."

Chapter Twenty-three

Still in Craig's arms, Summer turned. A woman stood in front of a bright red sports car at the curb. Overlarge sunglasses shielded her eyes and a portion of her forehead. Her hair, dyed ten different shades of blond, sat cropped close to her heart-shaped face. She was shorter than Summer, less curvy, definitely thinner, but the kind of thin indicative of an anorexic weight-loss method rather than a healthy diet. She wore a formfitting jacket in sage green atop a floral-print skirt, and a string of jade beads dipped to her chest in twin strands.

Tension radiated off Craig, sharp enough to draw blood. The woman, Chelsea, smiled in their direction, harder than diamonds. Summer would have to ease the pressure between them all.

"Just so you know, I could take her in a fight," she murmured to Craig with a saucy wink.

The joke worked. He relaxed, smiled. "I bet you can, but let's just see what she wants first, okay?" He faced his ex-wife with the same easygoing attitude, arm still casually draped around Summer's waist. "Chelsea, what can I do for you today?"

"I want to see my children, Craig."

He swept a hand toward the front door. "Go on in. Scott's inside playing video games. Maddie's at the park with my dad, and Nate should be home from summer camp in a few minutes."

She paused at the edge of the driveway. "Why isn't Scott at summer camp?"

"A growth plate fracture at baseball has kept him home for the last week or so," Summer said.

"A growth plate fracture? How exactly did my son sustain a growth plate fracture?"

"*Our* son collided with another player at third base." Craig's tone chilled.

"Another accident, Craig?"

Once again, Summer opted to jump in. "According to the ER doc, it's a fairly common injury. The best thing we did was take him directly to the emergency room rather than waiting. The leg will heal with no problem."

Chelsea pulled the glasses to the end of her nose and looked over the frames at her. "And you are . . . ?"

"Oops, sorry. I'm Summer. I'm . . ." She paused, looked at Craig. Oh, well. No help for it. Chelsea had seen him kissing her, so the nanny angle wouldn't hold much water. In fact, it would probably anger her more. "I'm Craig's girlfriend."

"And how involved is your girlfriend in our children's care, Craig?"

"It's not what you think, Chels."

"Umm, how about we table this discussion for now?" Summer interjected.

"She's my fiancée," Craig clarified.

Summer's jaw nearly fell to the sidewalk. As shocked as she was, though, the announcement stunned Chelsea even more. "Your fiancée?"

"Look, don't jump to conclusions right now, okay?" Craig said. "Spend some time with the kids, and when you're done, we'll go someplace quiet and talk. The three of us."

Summer shook her head. "The *two* of you. I don't belong in discussions involving your marriage or your children."

Chelsea scowled. "Oh, on the contrary. I think if you're going to marry Craig and be involved in the raising of my children, you should be there as well."

"Ordinarily I'd agree with you, Mrs. McIntyre, but what Craig has neglected to tell you is, I haven't said yes yet."

Chelsea's eyes narrowed on Summer for a long, intense

minute, and then her face broke into a grin. "I think I like you. It's too soon to tell, but you don't fall for Craig's charm. I respect that." She started walking toward the house and tossed over her shoulder, "Join us, Summer. After I've seen the kids."

Once Chelsea disappeared inside the house, Summer turned back to Craig. "Have you gone insane? Why on earth would you tell her I'm your fiancée?"

"Because I didn't want to have to explain how I fell in love with the nanny."

"I am *not* the nanny."

"You know what I mean. I don't want Chelsea to think I'm like Paul Hobart."

"And what happens when your kids tell her I'm not your fiancée, that I'm not even your girlfriend?"

"Ah, shinola!" He left her standing there, her question unanswered while he raced inside the house.

The door slammed behind him, and Chelsea turned to face him, a broad smile on her face. She sat on the couch, Scott pounding on the buttons of his gaming control beside her.

"I don't know where you met her, Craig, but I'm impressed." She gestured to the shelf against the wall where colorful boxes stored the toys that used to litter the now uncluttered carpet. "Her influence, I suppose."

"She's been good for us, Chels. The kids love her." He clamped his mouth shut, but the words had already escaped.

And of course, Chelsea leaped on his gaffe faster than a cheetah on a wounded hyena. "Is that so?" She turned back to Scott. "What do you think of your father's girlfriend, Scott?"

"Umm . . . ," Craig began.

Scott cut him off without ever pausing in his game. "Summer? She's cool. I miss the Pop-Tarts for breakfast, though."

"Oh? What do you have for breakfast instead?"

"Cereal, fruit, toast, omelets. Good stuff. The other day, we surprised her with French toast. But Dad made us cook with healthy stuff."

At Chelsea's puzzled look, Craig clarified, "Whole-wheat bread and egg substitute."

"Yo-ho, look who's here!" Dad announced as he walked into the living room with Maddie on his hip.

"Mommy!" Maddie shrieked and wiggled, arms outstretched toward Chelsea. The minute her grandfather put her down, she raced to Chelsea's side and buried her dark head in her mother's jacket.

"Hello, my angel," Chelsea greeted her as she smoothed the child's hair with the flat of her hand. "Look how big you're getting."

"Son," Dad said, "Summer told me to tell you she'll be outside weeding the back garden for a while."

"In other words," Chelsea remarked, "she's giving us some privacy. Classy lady, Craig."

"Nice change of pace," Dad retorted.

Craig shot him a warning glance. "Dad."

"Yeah, yeah," Dad muttered. "I think I'll go help Summer." He walked out just as Nate popped in. "Mom!"

Craig sank into the recliner and forced himself to relax. With Nate's arrival, the family circle was complete. More than ever, though, he wished he could be outside with Summer instead.

Summer yanked another dandelion out of the black mulch and tossed the weed into the bucket at her side.

"Craig's or Chelsea's?" a male voice said from behind her.

She looked up into Ken's smiling face. "What?"

He crouched beside her. "Dr. Jeff? That psychologist guy from the *Taking Sides* talk show? He once said that women often pull weeds as an outlet for their anger because it's the same kind of action as pulling someone's hair. So I'm asking you. Whose hair do you want to pull right now? Craig's or Chelsea's?"

Giggles overwhelmed her, and she fell back onto her butt, laughing. "Dr. Jeff said that, huh? Was that before or after he met my sister?"

He grinned. "Does it matter?"

"No. Definitely not." She sobered. "Your son just introduced me to Chelsea as his *fiancée*."

Understanding lit up his eyes. "Ah. Well, I *did* tell him life was too short to dillydally when it came to love."

"It's a huge hop from our first dance to wedding bells, don't you think?"

"He panicked. Chelsea has that effect on him, especially when she threatens to take the kids from him."

"You mean this isn't the first time she's threatened him?"

He gave a bitter laugh. "The first time was two weeks after he was awarded sole custody. She wanted to see them at three in the morning, before she and her husband flew off to some godforsaken place. When Craig wouldn't wake them up for her, she told him if she didn't have open access, she'd take them with her permanently." He shrugged. "Next thing I know, Craig's waking up the kids so they can say good-bye to their mother."

"That's horrible. How often does she threaten him like that?"

"It isn't what you think. I mean, yeah, that was a particularly mean episode, but it's not a normal occurrence. Up until recently, they've actually kept a civil peace between them for the kids' sakes. Till I had that second heart attack. Then Chelsea started making threats again. She said Craig couldn't handle the responsibility without help, and her husband had the financial means to make sure that the kids had a nanny, private tutors, and access to privileges Craig couldn't possibly give them. That's what sent him to that agency of your sister's."

"And why you were against it," she surmised.

"Yeah. I thought, what's the difference who's got 'em if the kids are being brought up by strangers? But I was wrong about hiring someone. About hiring *you*."

"Thank you."

"No, thank *you*. You brought laughter back to this house. And even better, you brought love. So if my son jumped the gun with you, don't hold it against him."

"I don't hold it against him. I just want time. For him, for me, for the kids."

"Too bad Chelsea doesn't see it that way." Craig's voice suddenly intruded into their conversation.

Summer looked up to see him striding toward them, a puzzled expression on his face. "Craig? Is everything all right?"

He spread his hands wide and shook his head. "I'm a little shell-shocked to discover that all three of my kids knew you and I were in love before we did. Even Maddie."

Ken folded his arms over his chest. "I told you that you guys were throwing off more sparks than Fourth of July fireworks." At Craig's icy glare, he backed away. "I think I'll go back inside. Make nice with Chelsea for a while." He made a quick retreat toward the back door.

Summer barely noticed his departure. Her focus remained pinned to Craig. "Is anything else bothering you?"

"Yeah," Craig replied. "Chelsea says if you agree to marry me, she'll stop threatening to take the kids away."

Good thing Summer was already seated on the ground. She didn't have any lower to go. Talk about emotional blackmail. "Craig, I—"

He held up a hand to stem her argument. "I told her we'd get married if and when we were ready. For love and not for legal purposes. In the meantime, she's welcome to join us for dinner, but this is the last time I intend to allow her to accompany the two of us on a date."

Logic fled. She widened her eyes, swallowed, tried to think of something to say. "You really said that?"

"Said every word and *meant* every word. She declined the dinner invitation, by the way. Says we deserve some alone time, and she wants time with the kids, so we all win. She also asked that we send her and Jake a wedding invitation. If and when we're ready."

Summer rose on shaky legs, brushed the dirt from her stained knees. "Craig, there's something you should know about me."

"You might still be in love with your ex? I know."

"No." She shook her head, then stopped to stare at him. "Why on earth would you think that?"

"The way you reacted when we saw him the other night at the home store. You practically fainted."

"But not because I still have feelings for him. Our marriage was over long before it actually ended." She took a deep, shuddering breath. Time to bare her darkest secret. Unable to face him, she dropped her gaze to the bucket of weeds. "I can't have children, Craig. A surgery I had a few years ago."

"Oh."

Her head snapped up. "'Oh'? Is that all you can say?"

"Well, yeah." He shrugged, but his face gave nothing away. "I mean, I get it now. You didn't react to seeing Brad. You were upset about his wife's pregnancy. The twitlet. I bet that kicked like an angry mule." At last, he smiled and exhaled a long breath. "That's a relief."

"Not to me. I'll never have a family."

"You will if you stay with me." He leaned closer, nuzzled her neck. "Three kids are enough, doncha think?"

Despite the sweet shivers rippling her flesh, she pushed him away. "We haven't even dated, and you're angling for marriage."

"No, I'm not. I'm just pointing out all the benefits. And if you can tear yourself away from the dirt around my house long enough, I'd like to take you out tonight. Just the two of us. Our first date. Well, second, if you count that dinner in my van. So what do you say?"

"I g-guess I should get cleaned up and change my clothes then. Where are we going?"

"For dinner? You choose. The place, the clothes, the food. All up to you. Everything is all up to you."

She arched a brow at him. "Even the wedding?"

He pulled her close, kissed her with enough emotion to make her dizzy. "We'll discuss that later. When we're *both* ready."

Cradling his face in her hands, she kissed him back. "No. When we're *all* ready."

Epilogue

Summer stood beside Lyn in the master bedroom of Snowed Inn Bed-and-Breakfast and marveled at the eternal beauty of this winter bride. Lyn's long-sleeved white satin gown boasted fur at the wrists and over the neckline. The corset-style waist belled to a generous double-peplum skirt edged in white lace embroidery highlighted by tiny red rosettes.

Lyn glowed with happiness and clasped her hands in front of her as if already wearing the fur muff that would complete the ensemble. "Well?"

"Perfect," Summer answered honestly. "Doug's going to fall in love all over again the minute he sees you."

Her smile nearly blinding, Lyn sighed her relief. "So, what's next for you?"

"On Monday, I fly to New York for the finishing touches on Duchess DeeLight's secret nuptials."

At their first meeting, when Daphne Beech had explained how the pop star wanted to be certain the press wouldn't discover her wedding plans until after she'd said "I do," Summer had convinced the professional assistant that holding the event in New York would throw everyone off the trail. So far she'd been successful in keeping the press from discovering that the Sands-Harrison wedding scheduled for the Plaza next week was actually for Duchess DeeLight and her longtime companion, film star Trent Dolby.

"That's not what I mean and you know it," Lyn huffed. "I'm talking about you and Craig. It's been long enough, don't you think? When are you going to put that poor man out of his misery?"

"Actually, I was thinking about making our engagement official tonight. If you don't mind."

"Mind?" Lyn clapped and hopped like a child, skirts rustling with each bounce. "I think it's a perfect idea!"

In the parlor, one floor below the master bedroom, Craig pulled April into a quiet corner beside the gaily decorated Christmas tree. "I want to show you what I bought Summer." He pulled a bright blue velvet box from his pocket and flipped the top to reveal a heart-shaped sapphire ring with square ruby ingots on each side.

April touched the gold band, smiled as the white lights of the tree glinted off the brightly colored gems. "Beautiful." She offered him a conspiratorial smile. "Does this mean what I think it means?"

"I want to make our engagement official tonight, after your sister's ceremony. Do you think Lyn and Doug will mind?"